STAB IN THE DARK

Nate considered himself to be fairly fleet of foot, but two of the Pawnees were as fast if not faster. A glance showed them hard after him and gaining. Neither let a shaft fly; evidently they intended to take him alive. Kuruk's doing, Nate suspected. Kuruk wanted to stake him out and torture him.

Nate tried to shake them. He cut back and forth at right angles. He weaved among benighted boles. The Pawnees not only kept up, they continued to gain. One of them called out to those behind.

Nate had lost his sense of direction. He wasn't sure which way he was running. He turned right.

From out of nowhere a warrior appeared. The man had a tomahawk and the instant he saw Nate, he raised it to cleave Nate's skull . . .

WILDERNESS #62:
THE TEARS OF GOD

David
Thompson

LEISURE BOOKS NEW YORK CITY

Dedicated to Judy, Joshua and Shane.
And to Beatrice Bean, with the most loving regard.

A LEISURE BOOK®

December 2009

Published by

Dorchester Publishing Co., Inc.
200 Madison Avenue
New York, NY 10016

ISBN 10: 0-8439-6262-3
ISBN 13: 978-0-8439-6262-8
E-ISBN: 978-1-4285-0782-1

Visit us online at www.dorchesterpub.com.

WILDERNESS #62:
THE TEARS OF GOD

Chapter One

The two men were grim with purpose. They came down out of the high country riding hard and fast. They didn't stop for a meal; they ate pemmican out of their parfleches as they rode. They slept only a few hours each night. Rest wasn't important, although they stopped when they had to for the sake of their mounts. Each time the younger man chafed at the delay.

They were a study in contrasts. The younger man's hair was raven black, while the older man's mane was as white as the snow that capped the highest peaks. Both wore buckskins, the younger man's decorated with blue beads by his Shoshone wife. The younger man wore an eagle feather in his hair; the older man covered his head with a beaver hat. Both had beards.

They were living armories. Each had a Hawken rifle, a brace of flintlock pistols, and knives. The younger man's knife was a bowie, the older man's a Green River blade. The younger man also had a tomahawk wedged under his belt. Their weapons had seen a lot of use.

They came down out of the miles-high mountains to the emerald foothills and through the foothills to the prairie. The younger man rode a bay, the older man a white mare. When the younger man once asked the older why he liked mares over any other kind of horse, the older man had replied with one of his impish grins, "I ride mares because it's nice to be in charge of a female for a change."

"I can savvy that," the younger man had replied.

"I'm married, too. But in all the years I've known you, you only ever ride white mares. Why not some other color?"

The older man had touched his own white mane. "I like the idea of snow on top and snow under me."

"That makes no kind of sense. What's the real reason?"

"I am practical, Horatio. A white horse is a lot easier to find when it strays off."

"Easier for hostiles to spot, too."

The younger man's name wasn't really Horatio. It was Nate King. His nickname was a token of how fond the older man was of the younger. A token, too, of the older man's intense passion for the works of the Bard of Avon. Shakespeare McNair owned one of the few volumes of his namesake's works west of the Mississippi River. He read the book religiously. He quoted it religiously, too, as he did now as they drew rein to let their animals rest.

" 'Ah, marry, now my soul hath elbow-room.' "

"That's a new one," Nate said as he took a spyglass from his parfleche.

"I was rereading *King John* when you came to fetch me," Shakespeare informed him.

"*King John*?" A grin spread under Nate's telescope. "Isn't that the boring one?"

Shakespeare stiffened in indignation. " 'What cracker is this same that deafs our ears with this abundance of superfluous breath?' " he quoted. "How dare you? The Bard never wrote a boring play in his life."

"I seem to recollect your wife saying she always finds you asleep in your rocking chair with the book in your lap."

"A pox on you. It's not the Bard who puts me to sleep, it's my years." Shakespeare put a hand to the small of his back. "I'm not as spry or as durable as I used to be."

"I hope to God I'm half as fit as you when I'm your age." Nate lowered the spyglass and frowned.

"Nothing?"

"Grass, grass, and more grass. I'd like the prairie more if it wasn't so god-awful flat."

"I've often thought the same thing myself," Shakespeare said with mock seriousness. "The good Lord should have broken the monotony. Say, with a volcano here or there."

Nate looked at him. "The things that come out of your mouth. That was plumb ridiculous."

They rode on. They saw few buffalo since most of the herds were to the south at that time of year. They did see a lot of deer and once they spied antelope and a black bear that ran off with that rolling gait bears have. Prairie dogs were common, and the two men wisely avoided the prairie dog towns for fear their horses might step into a burrow and break a leg.

That night they camped in a hollow. They didn't bother with a fire. They stripped and picketed their mounts, unrolled their blankets, and were ready for sleep.

Nate lay on his back, his hand under his head, gazing at the multitude of sparkling pinpoints in the firmament. "If anything has happened to her . . ." he said, and didn't finish.

Shakespeare was on his side, his back to his friend. Rolling over, he adjusted his blanket, then said, "She can take care of herself, Horatio. She's almost a grown woman."

"She's my daughter. And sixteen is still a girl. I love her more than I love all there is except my wife and my son and maybe you."

"I'm flattered," Shakespeare said dryly.

"I can't stand the thought of her being hurt, or worse," Nate confessed. "It eats at me like a termite eats at wood."

"You need to put it from your mind. Winona and you taught Evelyn well." Shakespeare paused. "'The quality of mercy is not strained. It droppeth as the gentle rain from heaven upon the place beneath.'"

"You're saying God would never let anything happen to her? I know better."

"Let's hope the Almighty didn't hear that," Shakespeare quipped. "You're getting cynical in your young age."

"I'm in my middle years and I've learned enough to know that rain falls on all of us."

"Haven't you heard, Horatio? Some folks say that raindrops are the tears of God. Anyway, she's with Waku and his family. They won't let anything happen to her."

"Tell that to a war party out to count coup. Or to a hungry griz. Or to any of the other thousand and one things that can do her harm."

"Keep this up and you'll have hair as white as mine."

Nate lowered his gaze from the heavens. "All I want is my daughter safe and sound. That's all I ask. She was supposed to be back by now." He closed his eyes and tried to put the worry from his mind. Maybe it was silly of him to get so wrought up, but he had seen too much of the brutal and cruel to take it for granted his daughter was safe.

At the crack of dawn they were up.

Shakespeare rose stiffly and winced. "I wish that book you have were true. I'd look up that doctor and have him operate on me."

About to roll up his blanket, Nate asked in puzzlement. "Which book?" He owned dozens. They filled a bookshelf in his cabin and were his most prized possessions.

"The one written by that lady, Shelley."

"Mary Shelley is her name. The book is called *Frankenstein*, or the *Modern Prometheus*." Nate remembered the sensation the book caused when it first came out.

"That's the one. It's too bad there isn't a real Dr. Frankenstein. I'd have him take the brain out of my body and plunk it in a younger one."

Nate laughed. "First volcanoes, now this. And to think you haven't had a drop of brandy."

"Wait until you're my age and then poke fun. It's not easy, getting old. It's not easy to have your body betray you. In your mind you can leap tall trees at a single bound, but in real life you can't hardly lift your feet over a log."

"Oh, please," Nate scoffed. "You have more vigor than men half your age. It wouldn't surprise me if you lived to be a hundred."

"'You prattle something too wildly,'" Shakespeare quoted, and grew serious. "We've been friends for so long, I don't blame you for taking it for granted I'll be around a good long while yet. But these old bones aren't what they used to be."

"Quit that kind of talk. Whether you have five years left or ten, the important thing is that you're not going to keel over this very moment."

Shakespeare clutched his chest and staggered, crying out, "'You spoke too soon, Horatio! My end is nigh.'"

"You're hopeless." Nate saddled the bay and was ready to ride out. He sat astride it, watching McNair tug on his cinch. "Tell me true. What do you rate our chances?"

"Of finding your sweet Evelyn alive and well?" Shakespeare rubbed his white beard. "About fifty-fifty, I'd say. The prairie takes up a lot of territory and there's just the two of us."

"I prefer it that way." Nate's wife had been all set to accompany him when their daughter-in-law, who was in the family way, came down sick. Nate's other half, who was well versed in herbs and healing, decided to stay and watch over her, much to the relief of their son, Zach.

"Are you afraid we'll run into trouble and you didn't want your lovely lady in harm's path?" Shakespeare smiled. "I admire the sentiment. That's why I asked my wife to lend yours a hand."

On they rode. While Nate had complained of the prairie being flat, it wasn't. Gullies, washes, and an occasional knoll or hill broke the sameness. About the middle of the morning they came to a shallow stream and drew rein.

"Another hour, maybe two, and we'll be at Bent's," Shakespeare said.

Nate couldn't wait. A former trading post, Bent's Fort had no connection with the military. Rather, it was a hub of commerce for a score of tribes both near and far. It was also a stopping point on the Santa Fe Trail and for those bound for Oregon Country.

"If there has been any word of her, they'll have heard it," Shakespeare confirmed.

"Let's hope," Nate said. Bent's was an information hub, as well. If a man wanted to know whether the Blackfeet were acting up, or how far afield the Sioux were raiding, or how many pilgrims were with the last wagon train bound for the Willamette Valley, all he had to do was ask at Bent's.

"Did you hear something, Horatio?"

Nate was so absorbed in worry over Evelyn he hadn't

been paying attention, a potentially fatal lapse in the wilderness. Hefting his Hawken, he raked the cotton-woods and undergrowth. A few sparrows were flitting about. Other than that, the vegetation was undisturbed.

"I could have sworn I did," Shakespeare said.

"What was it? A footstep? An animal? What?"

"I'm not sure."

Nate hid his surprise. His mentor was usually so alert and confident. "I'll have a look-see." It bothered him, all this talk of old age and dying. It was unlike McNair to brood. He made up his mind to have a long talk with him after they returned to King Valley.

The sudden snap of a twig brought Nate up short. Here he was, making the worst mistake a man could in the wilds: letting himself be distracted when there might be hostiles or a wild beast about. He wedged the Hawken to his shoulder and made ready to shoot.

Off in the brush something moved, something big, its silhouette a dark shadow against the backdrop of green. Nate hoped to God it wasn't a hostile on horseback or a griz. He'd had his fill of fighting both. Back when he'd first come West to trap beaver, griz-zlies were everywhere. He'd happened to tangle with one, and a Cheyenne warrior who witnessed the clash gave him the name by which all the tribes now knew him: Grizzly Killer.

The silhouette moved.

Nate held still. The shadow darkened, a sign it was coming toward him, and the next instant the creature stepped into view.

Chuckling, Nate let the Hawken's muzzle dip. "I don't see many of your kind this low anymore."

The cow elk stared at him without concern. Slowly, lazily, she munched and moved off.

Nate turned back. He was glad it hadn't been a

hostile. He would rather avoid running into one if he could help it. The problem was, a lot of tribes regarded whites as invaders, to be exterminated every chance they got. The Blackfeet, the Piegans, the Bloods, the Sioux, all were determined to drive the white man out. Not the Shoshones, though. His wife's people had always been friendly to whites, so much so, they adopted him into the tribe when he took Winona to be his wife.

It was strange how life worked out, Nate reflected. When he was growing up in New York he'd never imagined that one day he would live in the Rocky Mountains and call them his home. He'd never imagined a beautiful Indian woman would claim his heart, or that they would have two children, a boy and a girl, who grew to be the apples of his eye.

Ahead was the spot where they had stopped.

Shakespeare was standing near the horses, holding the reins to the white mare.

"It was an elk," Nate said. He started to go around the mare to his bay but stopped when he saw his friend's expression. "Something the matter?" he asked, and looked in the direction Shakespeare was looking.

There were four of them. Swarthy warriors with long oval faces, their black hair parted in the middle and hanging past their shoulders on either side. Instead of buckskins they wore long tunics and knee-high moccasins. They also favored shell earrings. Bone-handled knives hung from sheaths on their hips and quivers were across their backs. All four had short bows fitted with sinew strings. All four had notched arrows to the strings and pulled the strings back to their cheeks.

"Have a care, Horatio," Shakespeare cautioned. "We don't want to provoke them if we can help it."

Nate froze. He could have shot one or two, but at that range the others wouldn't miss. "Let's try talking to them and show them we're friendly."

The next instant the foremost warrior took a step and trained the barbed tip of his arrow on Nate's chest.

Chapter Two

•

The tapestry of life in the wilderness was woven of strands of both serenity and savagery. Times without counting Nate's life had hung in the balance. It might be hostiles, it might be a marauding griz, it might be Nature's tantrums or a menace as commonplace as a rattlesnake. It had happened so often in the past that when it happened in the present, he was seldom prone to panic. He felt fear, yes. He felt anxiety. But panic hardly ever.

Nate didn't panic now. He met the gaze of the warrior with the arrow pointed at him. Ever so slowly, he raised his right hand, empty, as high as his neck. Then he slowly closed it, held his first two fingers straight up, and brought his hand in front of his face. It was sign language for "friend."

The warrior studied Nate as if trying to decide whether to believe him. Lowering the bow, the man eased up on the string, raised his right hand, and mimicked Nate. He said something in a tongue Nate was unfamiliar with.

Shakespeare let out a long breath of relief. "Thank goodness. They thought we might be scalp hunters."

"You speak their language?" Nate marveled. He had lost count of how many his friend knew. As one of the first white men to roam the vast lands west of the Mississippi, McNair had run into more tribes than practically any other white man alive.

"Barely at all," Shakespeare responded. "But I know

the tribe. They're called the Pend d'Oreilles. They come from up near where my wife's tribe lives, the Flatheads."

"That's a far piece." Nate saw that the other warriors were lowering their bows and noted that each kept his arrow nocked to the string.

"They only get down this way once a year or so," Shakespeare said.

"What are they doing here?"

"What else? They've come to trade at Bent's." Shakespeare resorted to sign language, and the warrior who had pointed his bow at Nate replied in kind.

Nate knew sign as well as his friend did. He translated the answer out loud, "They have come for guns and steel knives if they can get them, and have brought furs and shells to trade." It was always the way, Nate reflected. Contact with whites stirred a desire for the white man's weapons. Bows and lances weren't enough when warriors had seen what guns could do. "Why in the world did they think we were scalp hunters?"

Shakespeare posed the question in sign. The answer provoked a frown. "You just saw. He says they met some Crows who warned them there are scalp men hereabouts."

"That's ridiculous." Nate was aware that lifting hair had been a common practice back East, but that was long ago.

"They say the Crows heard it from the Cheyenne who heard it from a band of Pawnees."

Nate scratched his chin. "What do you make of it? Do you believe them?"

Shakespeare nodded at the Pend d'Oreilles. "*They* believe it and that's what counts."

The leader went on at some length.

"He's sorry for disturbing us," Nate translated. "That's

awful decent of him. But that business about scalp hunters is far-fetched."

The leader let out a sharp cry. It wasn't a war whoop; it was a signal to the rest of his party. Out of the trees filed eight more warriors leading their horses and pack animals.

Nate was doubly glad he hadn't tried to fight his way out. He'd be bristling with arrows right about now. "Do we offer to ride with them or go on alone?"

Shakespeare put the question to them in sign. The leader answered that they would be happy to have the two white men ride with them.

Although Nate couldn't recall hearing tell of any instance where the Pend d'Oreilles killed whites, he wasn't entirely comfortable riding at the head of the band with all those bows at his back. He kept shifting and looking back.

Finally Shakespeare chuckled and said, "You'll give yourself a crick in the neck if you keep doing that."

"Do you trust them not to kill us if they have the chance?"

"Lordy, you have a suspicious nature."

"I just like to breathe."

"They could have done it back there at the creek if they wanted."

"That doesn't mean they might not try now."

" 'By my troth,' " Shakespeare resorted to the Bard, " 'a man can die but once. We owe God a death. I'll ne'er bear a base mind, an't it be my destiny.' "

"You're saying I worry too much."

Beaming, Shakespeare bent toward Nate and clapped him on the shoulder. "You're learning, Horatio. There's hope for you yet."

To Nate's considerable relief, the Pend d'Oreilles didn't badger them with questions about white ways.

Some tribes would. To them the white man was a per-
plexing mystery. The things most Indians held dear,
the white man didn't. The things that white men held
dear, the Indians couldn't understand. Especially the
whites' lust for money and desire to possess land was
another. Many tribes, like his adopted people the Shoshones, considered the land as there for all to use, hu-
mans as well as wildlife. The concept of owning it was
added proof that whites had their heads in a whirl.

The two hours seemed a lot longer, but at last the
winding Arkansas River came into view. The high
adobe walls of Bent's Fort were bathed in the afternoon sun. Nothing short of a cannon could break those
walls down. They were impervious to lances and arrows and immune to fire. Small wonder that hostiles
seldom attacked.

Nate had been here often. He was always impressed
by its size: almost one hundred and eighty feet from
front to back and nearly one hundred and forty feet
from side to side.

The Pend d'Oreilles drew rein a hundred yards out.
Indians were permitted into the post only at certain
times and kept under close watch. Whites could enter
any time but first had to go up to a gate in the south
wall and wait while they were scrutinized through a
porthole. The Bent brothers and their partner, Ceran
St. Vrain, took every precaution.

No sooner did Nate come to a stop than the porthole
opened and a voice thick with a brogue declared, "As I
live and breathe, it's Nate King, himself." The bar on the
inside rasped and the gate was hauled open, revealing a
young man with a bristly red beard and a knot of red
hair.

"It's been a while, Finnan," Nate greeted him.

"That it has," the Irishman agreed, all smiles. "I

haven't set eyes on you since you had your dispute with that horrible Jackson fellow and blew out his wick."

Nate didn't need the reminder.

Finnan flashed his teeth at McNair. "And who might this ancient gentleman with all the wrinkles be?"

Shakespeare's head snapped up. "Who are you calling ancient, you danged infant?"

"Here, now. Don't take that tone. I was being friendly, is all."

"I'll friendly you," Shakespeare said, and launched into another quote. " 'I find the ass in compound with the major part of your syllables.' "

"Huh?" Finnan said.

" 'Peas and beans are as dank here as a dog, and that is the best way to give poor Jade the bots.' "

"Huh?" Finnan said again.

" 'Zounds. I was never so bethumped with words since I first called my father's brother dad.' "

"What language is that you're speaking, old man? It sounds like English and yet it's not."

" 'You are duller than a great thaw.' "

"I understood that one, I think," Finnan declared, "and if I understood it correctly, I resent it." He glanced at Nate. "Is your friend drunk? Is that it?"

Nate was shaking with suppressed mirth. "Finnan, allow me to introduce my best friend in all creation. You are talking to none other than Shakespeare McNair."

"The saints preserve us!" the younger man blurted, and stepped to the mare. "I've heard so much about you, sir. You're as famous as Jim Bridger and Joseph Walker. It's an honor to finally meet you."

Shakespeare had raised a hand and was about to deliver another bombastic quote. "It is, is it?"

"Yes, indeed. They say you were the first white man to ever set foot in the Rocky Mountains."

"Not quite, but I was a close second. Or possibly third."

"May I shake your hand? I can't wait to tell everyone. I can hardly believe my luck."

"There's hope for you, after all," Shakespeare said, and leaning down, he offered his hand. "But take heed, boy. When you meet a person my age, the last thing you want to do is remind him of his years."

"Oh, I understand, sir. I'm sorry I did that. It's just that I've never met anyone as old as you before."

Nate snorted.

" 'This is the very coinage of your brain,' " Shakespeare said with a sigh.

"Huh?"

"Nothing. Stand aside so we can enter. I feel myself in serious need of hard liquor." Shakespeare gigged the mare and rode through the gate, casting a dark glance at Nate. "One word of this to my wife and I'll have your guts for garters."

"Now, now," Nate responded. "She is entitled to laugh the same as the rest of us."

Raising his face to the heavens, Shakespeare declared, " 'There's many a man that hath more hair than wit.' Was that a jest on your part or do you just like hair?"

Nate went to follow him.

"Does he always talk like that?" Finnan asked.

"There are days when I think he must have talked like that in the cradle," Nate said, and tapped his heels to the bay. Nothing much had changed since he last visited Bent's. The post was quieter than normal, in part because no wagon trains were there.

Nate crossed the compound and drew rein next to

McNair in front of the trading room just as the door opened.

"As I live and breathe, Nate and Shakespeare. I've missed you, my friends." Ceran St. Vrain emerged, his aristocratic features lit by a warm smile. He was dressed in the best of fashion, his hair neatly slicked, his boots polished.

"Ceran de Hault de Lassus de St. Vrain," Shakespeare said. "It is a joy for this old coon to set eyes on you again."

St. Vrain chuckled. "McNair, you are the only person alive who ever uses my full name, and how in the world you remember it is beyond me."

"His memory is formidable," Nate praised his friend. He had long been astounded by Shakespeare's ability to quote the Bard at will.

The three shook, and Ceran said, "How is it you're here? You can't be out of supplies so soon."

Nate's good humor evaporated like fresh rainwater under a hot sun. "I'm looking for my daughter."

"Evelyn? Yes, she was here some weeks ago with that family of Indians from the East you let settle in your valley. I'm afraid my memory isn't the equal of McNair's. What are they called again?"

"Nansusequas," Nate answered. "Wakumassee is the father. From what I gather, he took them off to hunt buffalo." Nate wished he had been home when they decided to go, but he'd been in St. Louis having his rifle repaired by the Hawken brothers.

"I seem to remember your daughter telling me that." Ceran stopped. "They haven't returned?"

"No." The simple word tore at Nate's heartstrings like his keen-edged bowie. "They've been gone much too long."

"We'll find them, Horatio," Shakespeare vowed. "If we have to scour the prairie from end to end, we'll find them."

Nate refused to delude himself. The plains were vast beyond measure, stretching countless leagues from Canada to Mexico and from the Mississippi to the Rockies. Granted, he doubted that Evelyn and Waku had gone that far, but the task was still daunting. "Have you heard anything?" he asked St. Vrain. "Has anyone seen them? Has there been any word at all?"

"Would that there had." Ceran's broad brow furrowed. "I'll be more than happy to organize a dozen men to go with you. You can cover that much more ground in much less time."

Nate was tempted. Time was crucial. The longer it took, the less the odds of finding them. "Have there been any reports of the Blackfeet down this way? Or have the Sioux been on the prowl?"

"The Sioux are always on the prowl," Ceran said, and caught himself. "But no, nothing recent. The Sioux are staying up in their Black Hills, and the Blackfeet haven't sent a war party this far south since last summer."

"When you talked to her, did she happen to mention which way they were headed?" Nate asked.

"East, as I recall. I reminded her that most of the buffalo are to the south, but she was confident they . . ." Ceran gave a slight start and visibly blanched. "Oh, my word."

"What?"

"I just remembered."

"What?" In his excitement, Nate gripped St. Vrain's arms. "Don't keep me in suspense."

Ceran swallowed and forced a smile. "Calm down.

As you say, it's a vast prairie. It's unlikely they ran into them."

"Ran into who?"

"There's been word," Ceran began, "of trouble to the east. The first accounts were sketchy. I thought it couldn't be true, but then other reports reached my attention."

Nate was practically beside himself. "Reports of *what*?"

"Of a band of white scalp hunters who have been killing and scalping every Indian they come across."

"God, no," Nate said. It was true, then. And it meant his friends the Nansusequas—and his daughter—were in deadly danger.

Chapter Three

A map never gave a true sense of scale. It said X was five hundred miles from Y, or that at its closest point the Mississippi was nine hundred miles from the Rockies. A person could picture it in his head, but the picture never matched the reality.

This was what went through Nate King's mind as he hurried eastward from Bent's Fort on the morning of the sixth day out. There was so *much* prairie; a sea of it, flowing on, mile after mile after mile. Finding someone in that immense ocean of grass was akin to looking for a tiny bit of driftwood in the middle of the Atlantic or the Pacific.

Nate thought of Evelyn and choked down despair. Ceran St. Vrain had told them that the scalp hunters were ranging wide over the region, killing men, women, and even children and lifting their hair. The question Ceran couldn't answer was why they were so far north of their usual haunts. It was well known that Texas and the government down to Santa Fe both offered money for scalps. In Texas it was for Comanche hair. In New Mexico it was for Apache scalps. But Texas and Santa Fe were a thousand miles away.

Rumor had it that some scalp hunters weren't particular about whose hair they lifted. Some would scalp whites and Mexicans, too, so long as the hair could pass for Comanche or Apache. Nate suspected that the band doing the marauding had come north because it would be easy to fill their hair sacks to bulging and then take them to Texas or Sante Fe and claim thousands of dollars in bounty.

Nate couldn't see them lifting Evelyn's hair. Hers would never pass for an Indian's. But the Nansusequas with her had the kind of hair a scalp hunter would love. And if they killed Waku and his family, what might they do to Evelyn? They might not want a witness.

Again despair nipped at Nate and he pushed it back down. Suddenly he realized Shakespeare was calling his name and drew rein. "What is it?" he asked, turning in the saddle.

Shakespeare brought the mare to a stop and pointed. "You need to come out of yourself."

A mile to the northeast smoke curled to the sky, rising in gray coils like a thick snake climbing into the clouds.

"White men made that fire," Nate remarked. Indians invariably made their fires small so as not to give them away.

Shakespeare grunted in agreement. "Whoever they are, maybe they've seen Evelyn and Waku. We should pay them a visit."

It took all Nate's self-control not to push at a gallop. He had already been riding too hard for too long and his bay showed signs of flagging. He held to a quick walk, his insides churning.

"How are you holding up?" Shakespeare asked.

"I'm fine."

"You're a terrible liar, Horatio."

Nate rubbed his jaw and scowled. "I can't help it. I love that girl so much. It's hard being a parent, the hardest thing there is."

"If it will help, you can talk about it."

"All talking will do is make me feel worse." But Nate

couldn't keep it in. "We raise them and nurture them. We are there as they grow day by day. We grin at their antics and smile at their silliness and feel our hearts fit to burst when they hug us and tell us they love us. We do the best we can to make them ready for the world and one day they go off to take up their own lives and we pray to God nothing bad will happen to them."

"Evelyn didn't go off to live somewhere. She went buffalo hunting."

"We love them so much and it hurts that the world will do to them as it does to everyone. It will rip at them and claw at them and try to crush them and there's not a thing we can do."

Shakespeare chuckled. "Aren't you exaggerating just a tad?"

"You think it's funny, but it's not. Every parent's worst fear is that something terrible will happen to their children. It is the worst that can happen, even more than a wife or husband dying."

"Good Lord. For all we know, she's fine. Pull your-self together. Your fear is getting you carried away."

"I know," Nate said, and sighed. "I can't help it. It's like wrestling with your own heart."

"Sometimes I wish Blue Water Woman and I had been able to have children," Shakespeare said wist-fully. "But it wasn't meant to be."

They could smell the smoke now. A low rise hid the source. Nate placed his Hawken across his saddle, his thumb on the hammer, his finger on the trigger. Not all whites were friendly.

"I hear voices."

So did Nate. A lot of them, talking in low tones. He slowed as he neared the top of the rise and drew rein the moment he could see over so as not to show him-self before he was sure it was safe.

"By my troth," Shakespeare said. "Freighters, unless I miss my guess."

Nate came to the same conclusion. He counted ten wagons of the prairie schooner variety. All were red and blue and covered by arched canvas tops. The wagons had been drawn up in a circle, and close to thirty people were moving about or seated at the fire. The wagons hid some from his view. Oxen were being taken from their traces and horses had been gathered to one side. "Bound for Bent's Fort, I reckon."

"Let's ride down and introduce ourselves," Shakespeare suggested. "We never know. They might have word of Evelyn."

Nate slapped his legs and rode over the rise. Almost instantly a man with a rifle appeared, a sentry Nate hadn't noticed. The man hollered and all the men in the circle grabbed rifles and came to watch Nate and Shakespeare approach.

"They are well trained," Shakespeare remarked. "Whoever is in charge runs a tight train."

"I bet that's him there."

A broad man with bulging shoulders had stridden to the forefront. His big hands were on a pair of pistols. A short-brimmed hat crowned rugged features. From under it poked brown hair a shade darker than the several days' growth on his square chin.

"I've seen that redwood somewhere," Shakespeare said.

Nate brought the bay to a halt and nodded at the human tree. "Howdy. My name is Nate King. I'm—" He got no further. The man broke into a smile and many of the others glanced at one another and commenced to whisper.

"The Lord, He works in mysterious ways," intoned their captain. "I'm Jeremiah Blunt. This is my train and

these are my men. I can't tell you how pleased we are
to meet you."

"Why would that be?"

"We have something that belongs to you, in a man-
ner of speaking." Blunt chuckled, and turning his head,
raised his voice. "It's all right, girl. It's safe for you and
the others to show yourselves."

For one of the few times in his life Nate was struck
speechless when a squealing vision of budding
womanhood bounded toward him with glee writ all
over her.

"Pa! Pa! It's you!"

Nate vaulted down. No sooner did his feet touch the
ground than Evelyn flew into his arms and hugged
him close. Choking off a sob, she said softly, "You don't
know how happy this makes me."

Nate couldn't talk for the lump in his throat. He
closed his eyes and held her and his thankfulness
knew no bounds.

From around the wagons came five people dressed
in green buckskins: Wakumassee and his family.
Warm greetings were exchanged and then everyone
sat around the fire at Jeremiah Blunt's invitation and
over coffee Nate heard of how the scalp hunters had
chased his daughter and the Nansusequas and would
have slain them had it not been for the freighter
captain.

"I'm in your debt," Nate said, pumping the other's
hand. "Anything you want of me, any time, you have
only to ask."

"I'll keep that in mind."

Nate learned that the freighters had made for Bent's
Fort, only to be delayed by a Sioux war party.

"There must have been sixty or more," Blunt told
him. "I circled the wagons expecting an attack, but

they stayed out of rifle range. For ten days they rode around us and whooped and waved their weapons, but they never once came at us."

"The Lakotas aren't stupid," Shakespeare threw in.

"No, they are not," Blunt agreed. "Our rifles would have taken a fearsome toll. They held us there, maybe figuring to starve us or have us run low on water, until finally they lost interest and went elsewhere."

"I was awful glad," Evelyn said. "If they had caught Waku and his family and me alone . . ." She didn't finish.

"That makes twice you saved my girl's life," Nate said to Blunt.

"Thank the Lord, not me. We are all sparrows in His eyes."

The time passed so quickly that before Nate knew it, twilight was falling and Blunt's men were preparing supper. He drained his tin cup of coffee and said, "I take it you are on your way to Bent's Fort and after that Santa Fe?"

"You take it partly right," Blunt replied. "We were taking your daughter and her friends to Bent's. From there she said they could make it home safe by themselves. But it's not Santa Fe, after. Normally it would be, but this is a special trip."

"How so?" Shakespeare wondered.

Jeremiah Blunt regarded them thoughtfully. "From what I hear, hardly anyone knows the mountains better than you two. Is that right?"

Shakespeare shrugged. "I've lived out here longer than most, so naturally I know them pretty well. Horatio has been all over, too."

"Horatio?" Blunt repeated.

"His nickname for me," Nate explained. "From William Shakespeare's play *Hamlet*."

"Ah." Blunt grinned at McNair. "I've heard about your quirk. You are as devoted to the Bard as I am to my Bible."

"A man can be devoted to both," Shakespeare said.

"True." Blunt turned to Nate. "But my point in asking how well you know the mountains is that I am thinking of taking you up on your offer."

"I'm listening," Nate said. He would do whatever he could for this man. He owed him that.

Blunt swept a stout arm at the ring of wagons. "The freight I'm carrying has been bought and paid for by a group of Shakers. I gave them my word I would get their supplies to them and I always keep it."

"What are Shakers?" Evelyn asked.

"A religious order, you might say," Jeremiah Blunt answered. "They broke away from the Quakers some time back. For a while they were called the Shaking Quakers, but now it's just Shakers."

"What a funny name. Why would anyone call them that?"

"Because, girl, that's what they do. When they worship they dance and tremble and, well, *shake*. They call it growing close to their Maker. Others call it having fits."

"What do you say?"

"Judge not, girl, lest you be judged. They believe in the Lord and that's enough for me. But a lot of folks see it differently. They want nothing to do with them, which is why this group came West to start a new colony."

Nate had heard of them. Their full name, as he recollected, was the United Society of Believers in Christ's Second Appearing. They lived in communities or villages all their own and had little to do with the outside world.

Shakespeare cleared his throat. "A new colony, you say?"

"Yes. A place all their own, a valley. I've never been there. Their leader, the man who hired me, gave me a map, but it blew away one night when I was studying on how to get there." Blunt looked at Nate. "That's the favor I'd like to ask. Unknown territory is always full of hazards for my wagons. I'm hoping you can lead me there and save me a lot of trouble."

"Where, exactly?" Nate asked.

Blunt pointed to the northwest. "Up near the geyser country. The valley has a peculiar name, but their leader swears it's a new Eden."

"What name?"

"It's called the Valley of Skulls."

"Zounds," McNair said, and he did not sound pleased.

"What's the matter, Uncle Shakespeare?" Evelyn asked him. "Do you know of this place? You, too, Pa?"

Nate nodded.

"You look fit to choke," Blunt said to McNair. "What do you know that I don't? Why is it called the Valley of Skulls?"

"It sounds spooky," Evelyn said.

Nate waited with everyone else for his mentor to speak. He knew some of the valley's history but not all and he had long been curious.

"To the Indians the valley is bad medicine," Shakespeare began. "Not just to a few tribes, to *all* of them. Not one will go anywhere near it."

"That's partly why the Shakers picked it," Blunt said. "To be safe from hostiles. The other part is that the ground shakes from time to time, or so their leader told me. He heard about the valley from an acquaintance of John Coulter's."

Nate met Coulter once. Coulter had been with the Lewis and Clark expedition and stayed on exploring after the pair returned to the States. Coulter was the first white man to ever set eyes on the hot springs and geysers that became known as Coulter's Hell.

Blunt had gone on. "Their leader—his name is Lexington, Arthur Lexington—took it as an omen. The way he told it to me is that the shaking ground is a sign from heaven that the valley is sacred to the Lord, and what better place for a colony of Shakers to live?"

Evelyn fidgeted with impatience. "But no one has said why they call it the Valley of Skulls. Why won't the Indians go there?"

"Because, sweet angel," Shakespeare said somberly, "nearly everyone who does dies."

Chapter Four

The Shoshones, the Crows, the Nez Perce, and other tribes all had stories to tell about the Valley of Skulls. The stories varied as to the particulars, but all agreed on certain points.

Long ago the valley was inhabited by a long-nosed race who wore crude hides and carried clubs and lived in the many caves on the sides of the valley and preyed on the animals that roamed the valley floor. This was in the days before Coyote created the first true people, back when there were many large and unusual and marvelous animals unlike any that lived now.

Legend had it that when the early people tried to make friends with the Long Noses, the Long Noses rose up in fierce violence and drove the people out. As punishment, Coyote had the ground shake so hard that it killed all the Long Noses in their caves and all the strange animals on the valley floor.

For many moons the early people stayed away from the valley, but then several made bold to explore and were amazed at what they found. Everywhere there were skeletons, picked clean as if by a swarm of buzzards. Giant skulls gleamed white, skulls of creatures the early people had never seen. The stench was horrible. Not the smell of the bones but the smell of the air itself. It made the early people cough and choke. They quickly left, and after that the valley became known as the Valley of Skulls.

For ages now the neighboring tribes considered the valley bad medicine and tribal members were warned to stay out. A few hunters had strayed into it and never come out. Once a war party thought to use the valley as a shortcut to where they were going and only a few made it out alive. They reported that it was a vile place where the ground shook and strange fogs appeared.

All this went through Nate's mind as he listened to Shakespeare recount the legends.

"Remarkable," Jeremiah Blunt said. "But from what I understand, the Shakers have been living there awhile now and not had any problems. So what do you say, King? Are you willing to guide my train?"

Nate would rather not. He would rather head for his own valley with Evelyn and his friends. He would rather be safe and snug in his cabin with his wife and family. But he owed this man, and he replied, "It will take us weeks, but I can get you there."

"Oh, goody!" Evelyn exclaimed in delight. "I want to see this mysterious valley for myself."

"You're not going anywhere near it," Nate said.

"What? Why not?"

"Because your uncle Shakespeare is taking you and Waku and his family straight home."

"Aw, Pa." Evelyn didn't hide her annoyance. "It will be an adventure."

Shakespeare gave a rumbling laugh. "Haven't you had enough excitement of late? You were lucky to escape those scalp hunters. You shouldn't push your luck, little one."

Evelyn wouldn't let it drop, but Nate refused to give in. That night after supper, he got up to stretch his legs and came on his daughter and Waku's son, Degamawaku, over by the horses. They didn't notice him and were talking in hushed tones. He didn't want Evelyn to think he was snooping, so he started to back away.

"It wrong not tell," Dega said.

"Trust me on this," Evelyn responded.

"It wrong," Dega insisted.

Nate saw his daughter clasp Dega's hand.

"You have a lot to learn about white ways. There is a time and a place, and this isn't it."

Then Nate was out of earshot. He wondered what that was about and figured if it was anything important Evelyn would inform him. She rarely kept secrets.

The next morning Shakespeare pumped Nate's hand and said, "Don't fret, Horatio. I'll watch over her as if she were my own. I'll get her to your cabin and she'll be waiting there when you return."

"I know I can count on you." There was no one Nate trusted more.

Evelyn was still miffed. She hugged him and said, "I wish you would change your mind, Pa. I'll behave. I'll do whatever you tell me to. Only I'd really love to see this valley."

"No, and that's final."

Still, it tugged at Nate's heartstrings to stand there and smile and wave as they rode off.

"I thank you for this," Jeremiah Blunt said at his elbow. "As a father, I know what you must be going through."

"I gave you my word."

"A man after my own heart," Blunt said, and smiled. "Now suppose we get under way? It will help if you keep busy."

Nate didn't have much to do. He saddled the bay and was ready to ride well before the oxen were hitched and Blunt gave the order for the wagons to move out. He admired how the men bustled about and

how efficiently they followed orders. There wasn't a
slackard in the bunch. Blunt had a lot to do with that;
he gave a command once, in a quiet tone, and the men
leaped to obey.

At midday, when they stopped to rest the teams,
Nate mingled with the freighters. There were twenty-
two, a tough, taciturn bunch. They took turns either
handling a wagon or riding flank and rear guard. To a
man, they bristled with weapons and when riding
guard were always alert.

Nate commented at one point on how they worked
so well together and a wiry bundle of vigor by the
name of Haskell spat a wad of tobacco and said, "We
have all been with the captain for more than a few
years. He hires only the best and expects the best of us."

"You admire him, then."

"I'd die for him," Haskell declared, "as would any
man jack in this whole outfit."

The rest nodded or said that yes, they would.

"He sure inspires loyalty," Nate remarked.

"Mr. King, you don't know the half of it. Jeremiah
Blunt is the cream of the captains. He treats us fair and
pays us well and only asks that we do our jobs."

Nate came to learn that Haskell and a man called
Trimble were Blunt's lieutenants. Another bull-whacker
worked as the wrangler and saw to the horses. There
was a cook and swampers and others. Gradually they
warmed to him, so that by the second week they were
treating him as one of their own.

Jeremiah Blunt commented on that one evening.
"The men have taken a liking to you, King. They say
you aren't what they expected."

"How so?"

"They haven't gotten to know many mountain
men. Oh, we see your kind from time to time, but we

seldom go up into the mountains and mountain men seldom come down from the heights. To be honest, I am a bit surprised, myself."

"I don't savvy."

"To be frank, your kind have a reputation for being—how shall I put this—crude."

"My mother raised me to have manners," Nate joked.

"It's not just that. The stories we've heard, we thought mountain men never take baths and vomit obscenities with every other word out of their mouths."

Nate had often wondered how the mountaineers, as his kind liked to call themselves, came to be so widely regarded as smelly, foulmouthed brutes. He suspected it started back in the trapping days. One newspaper, as he recalled, had described trappers as "young and feckless savages who gather once a year to drink, brawl, and womanize." While it was true the annual rendezvous had been one long celebration, the portrait painted wasn't precise. For most of the year, the trappers worked their fingers to the frigid bone, laying and raising traps from cold streams and skinning and curing hides. During the winter months when many of the waterways were frozen and the beaver stayed warm in their lodges, the trappers stayed warm in their cabins and spent much of their time reading and discussing what they read. The Rocky Mountain College, as it was known. Nate had many fond memories of long and deep talks about everything under the sun. Sure, there were trappers whose only interest was drinking and brawling and who fit the common notion of being rough-hewn barbarians, but most were hardworking, earnest souls, and Nate had been proud to know them.

"McNair and you both go against the grain," Blunt was mentioning. "You are men of intelligence."

"I thank you for the compliment," Nate responded, although he certaintly wasn't as smart as Shakespeare. For that matter, he wasn't as smart as his wife, Winona, who picked up new tongues as easy as could be and spoke English more fluently than he did.

Just then the cook came up and reported to Blunt they were running out of fresh meat. Every few days men were picked to go hunt and they rarely returned empty-handed.

"That's where I can help the most," Nate offered. "I'll do your hunting for you." He was good at tracking and knew the habits of the wild creatures better than most.

"I accept," Blunt said. "Only you're never to go anywhere alone. I have a rule to that effect and no one is to break it. There must always be someone to watch your back."

"I've been living in the wilderness for years. I can take care of myself," Nate assured him.

"No doubt you can, but a rule is a rule. There are no exceptions. We do what is safe." Blunt added with considerable pride, "I've never lost a man and I don't intend to lose one on this run."

Haskell was assigned to go with Nate the next morning. They roved ahead of the train across open prairie. Now and again Nate swept the horizon with his spyglass, but game proved scarce.

"We'll reach the South Platte in a day or two," Nate commented at one point. "From there we'll strike out for the North Platte and then it's over South Pass and on into the geyser country."

"What sort of hostiles are there to worry about?"

Haskell asked. "On the Santa Fe Trail it's Comanches and Apaches."

"To the northeast are the Sioux, who will kill you as soon as look at you," Nate enlightened him. "To the north is the Blackfoot Confederacy. The Blackfeet, the Piegans, the Bloods, have all been out for white hide ever since Meriwether Lewis shot a Blackfoot years back."

"They sure hold a grudge," Haskell said.

"To the west are the Utes. They don't like whites much, either. They tried making peace once, but the man the whites picked to parley shot the Ute chief from his horse."

"Why in hell did he do that?"

"He hated the Utes for killing his brother. Ever since, the Utes haven't trusted us worth a lick."

"I can't say as I blame them."

Nate didn't mention that the Utes trusted him. He had earned their trust the hard way, by proving he was worthy. Once, he brokered a truce between the Utes and another tribe. Another time, he hunted down and slew a grizzly that had been raiding Ute villages.

"You like it out here, don't you? The wilds, I mean?"

"That I do," Nate affirmed with a bob of his chin. "The free life agrees with me."

"I'm as free as you, but I'd never live where there are so many savages out to lift my hair and beasts that would like to rip my guts out and eat them."

"You're wrong there," Nate said.

"Wrong where?"

"About being as free as me. In the mountains a man lives as he pleases. There aren't any laws. There aren't any politicians to say 'do this' or 'do that.' There are no taxes or tolls to pay. We do what we want when we want. We let no one impose on us, ever, and are beholden to no one unless we want to be."

Haskell shrugged. "So what if there are laws I have to live by? They're for the good of all."

"So they say. But every law is another bar in the invisible prison that pens men in."

"You have a peculiar outlook."

Nate wondered. Most men were like the freighter lieutenant, content to live as others wanted them to. He couldn't stand being told what to do. To him, the free life was the only life worth living.

"Say, what are those?" Haskell abruptly asked, and pointed.

Far to the north stick figures moved. Nate drew rein and brought out his spyglass. "Riders," he announced. "Ten or more." He could make out lances and shields. "Indians."

"What tribe are they from?"

"I can't tell at this distance."

Haskell gazed about at the flat grassland. "There's nowhere to hide. Do we run for it?"

Nate adjusted the telescope, seeking to see the warriors better. "They're heading east, not in our direction." He lowered the spyglass. "We should be fine right where we are."

"Why have they stopped?"

Nate looked. The entire band had indeed halted. He raised the spyglass and was disconcerted to discover the warriors had turned their mounts and were staring to the south—straight at Haskell and him.

"Have they seen us?"

Nate lowered his telescope again. A splash of sunlight off the brass tube explained what had happened. "Oh, hell."

"That's the first time I've heard you cuss. You have me worried, mountain man."

Nate was growing concerned, too. The warriors were galloping toward them. Each had a shaved head except for a spine of hair down the middle. "They're Pawnees."

"Is that good or bad?"

"It depends. Sometimes the Pawnees are friendly."

"And the other times?"

"Let's just say we need to keep our wits about us if we want to go on breathing."

Chapter Five

The exact number was eleven. All were stocky and powerfully built. They slowed and spread out as they neared Nate and the bull-whacker. Haskell nervously fingered his rifle and said, "I don't get why we're not riding like our backsides are on fire."

"They'd catch us," Nate predicted.

"Then shoot a few now before they get too close."

"That would only make the rest mad." Nate shook his head. "We'll do this my way. Follow my lead. Don't talk. Just keep an eye on them. If they act as if they're going to stick us with their arrow and lances, we'll fan the breeze."

"You're taking an awful gamble."

"I know," Nate admitted. He reined the bay broadside to the Pawnees and held his Hawken across his saddle so the muzzle pointed at them. "Remember. I do the talking."

"Fine by me," Haskell said. "I don't speak a lick of Injun. Not even that hand talk they use."

Nate supposed it was normal for a freighter not to make the effort. For him it had been essential he learn sign language.

"King?"

"Hush now."

The warriors were soon upon them. Slightly ahead of the rest rode one who carried himself with an air of authority. When he drew rein so did the rest. No weapons were brandished, but they held them ready.

Nate was set to explain that Haskell and he weren't enemies and it would be best for everyone if they went their separate ways when the apparent leader addressed him in English.

"White man."

"*Chaticks-si-Chaticks*," Nate said. It was the Pawnee name for their people. It meant "men of men," which showed their opinion of other tribes.

The leader's surprise showed. "You know of us? Do you speak our tongue?"

"Only a few words," Nate admitted. "But it is good you know mine so I can tell you we want no trouble with the *Chaticks-si-Chaticks*."

"Only one of us may call another of us by that name," the warrior said stiffly. "You may call us what the rest of your kind do."

"Very well, Pawnee," Nate said. "How is it you speak my language?"

"I speak English. I speak French. I speak Spanish. How many tongues do you speak?" The warrior didn't wait for an answer. He sat taller and and thrust out his chest. "I am a Chaui. Do you know what that means, white man?

Nate was aware that the Pawnees were made up of four groups. The Chaui were the leaders. "How are you called?"

"I am Kuruk," the warrior proudly declared. "It means 'bear.'"

"I have an Indian name," Nate revealed, and had to smile at the irony. "I'm called Grizzly Killer."

Kuruk gave a start. "The white Shoshone?"

"You have heard of me?"

"I have seen you. But it has been so long I did not recognize you."

Nate racked his brain and said, "If we've met it is news to me. Your face isn't familiar."

"Think back, white man," Kuruk said harsly. "Think back seventeen winters. You were a guest in a village of my people."

Nate was jolted by the memory. He hadn't been a guest; he had been a virtual prisoner, a pawn in a struggle for power between a medicine man and a chief. "I remember being there, but I don't remember you."

"Do you remember a warrior called Red Rock?" Kuruk asked bitterly. "He was my uncle."

Nate never forgot a man he killed. Sometimes at night he woke up drenched in sweat from dreams where he relived the killings. "He was trying to stab me. I defended myself."

Kuruk seemed not to hear. "I was a boy then. I loved my uncle very much. He gave me a pony. He treated me as his own son." Kuruk glared at Nate. "It made me mad that his killer got away."

Haskell said, "Uh-oh."

"Now here you are," Kuruk continued, and smiled coldly. "Tirawa has brought you to me after all these winters."

Nate had not heard that word in a long time. Tirawa was the Pawnee god, the being who created the Pawnees and taught them to hunt and to make fire and gave them their language. Tirawa, who demanded regular human sacrifice in order for the Pawnees to reap the god's blessings. "I hope we have no quarrel, you and I. As you say, it was long ago."

Kuruk's dark eyes flitted from Nate's face to the Hawken across Nate's saddle and then back again. "Long ago," he repeated. He said something in Pawnee and the others studied Nate intently.

"They're fixing to lift our hair," Haskell whispered. "Let's get the hell out of here."

Nate raised the barrel just enough that the muzzle was pointed at the Chaui. They all heard the click of the hammer. "Do we have a quarrel?"

For seconds that seemed like minutes, Kuruk just sat there. Then his smile slowly widened and became even colder. Hate he couldn't hide was in his eyes and his tone as he said, "We have no quarrel, Grizzly Killer. We will let you go in peace." So saying, he reined sharply around and the rest followed suit. Tendrils of dust rose from under the pounding hooves of their mounts as they rode off to the northeast. Not one looked back.

Haskell let out a long breath. "Whew. I thought for sure this was the day I'd meet my Maker."

"He lied," Nate said.

"Pardon?"

"You saw. He'll never forgive or forget. He wants me dead."

"Then why didn't he do it here and now? There were enough of them, they could have rubbed us out without half trying."

"I would have shot him and he knew it." Nate had met men like Kuruk before. They never struck unless they had an edge. "We must warn your boss. We're heading back."

"Those red devils would be fools to attack our wagons," Haskell said. "We'd shoot them from their horses before they got close enough to loose an arrow."

Nate reined the bay around. "Only if they attack in the open in broad daylight. But they're not stupid. They'll pick you off from ambush one by one until there are more of them than there are of you and then they'll close in."

"Captain Blunt is too smart to let that happen."

"Let's hope."

The train had covered barely two miles. Jeremiah Blunt listened to Nate's account and then rubbed the stubble on his chin.

"Well, now. I didn't count on this. I asked a favor of you thinking you could be of help, not a hindrance." Blunt held up a hand when Nate went to respond. "Don't take me wrong. I don't hold it against you. How were you to know there were Pawnees within a hundred miles? We'll take extra precautions from here on out."

"I could go," Nate proposed. "I doubt Kuruk will cause you trouble if I'm not with your train."

"Alone you are easy pickings. No, it's wisest you stay with us. If the Pawnees want you, they'll have to work at it."

"I'd rather none of your men were killed on my account."

"That's decent of you, but we're none of us yellow. I don't hire cowards. We have twenty-three rifles plus extras and forty-six pistols, enough to stand off a war party ten times the size of this Kuruk's."

Nate had to admit that with the wagons circled, the freighters could put up a formidable defense. He didn't like the notion, though, of being dogged by a warrior out for revenge. He mulled it over the rest of the day and by supper had come to a decision. He walked to the fire where Blunt was pouring coffee, held out his own tin cup, and hunkered next to the captain. "I have a proposition for you."

"To use your own words, I'd rather you didn't."

Nate looked at him in surprise. "You haven't heard it."

"I don't need to." Blunt propped an elbow on a knee.

"I've taken your measure. You, sir, are a man who always does what he thinks is right, and hang the consequences. Am I correct?"

"Most men do the same," Nate said.

"No, they don't. Too many look out for themselves. They put their own interests before everyone else and they don't care who is hurt by it. They're petty and mean and can't ever talk well of anyone else. They carp and they whine and they stab others in the back."

Nate laughed. "You don't have a very high opinion of your fellow man."

"No, I do not." Blunt sipped and scowled. "I wish it were otherwise. When I was young I did. I lived and breathed the Bible and thought everyone did the same. I believed, truly believed, that all men were brothers and all women sisters and that all it took for all of us to get along was for all of us to care for one another." His scowl deepened. "I was a fool."

"You can't be faulted for thinking the best of everyone."

"Yes, I can," Blunt said severely. "My head was in the clouds. I took it for granted everyone was like me when they weren't. That's the key, you see. We are all of us different. I have made no secret of the fact I am a Christian. I confess to you now that the great shock of my life was to realize that many, or dare I say most, of my fellow men are not as I am and have no real interest in being so. They are content to go through life being selfish and vain and give little thought if any to their Maker." Blunt shook himself. "But to get back to you. I suspect you have taken the notion to go out after this Kuruk before he attacks my train. Am I correct or not?"

"You are." It dawned on Nate that here was a man every bit as shrewd as Shakespeare and every whit as smart as Winona. "I intend to slip away in the middle of the night. There's less chance the Pawnees will be watching us then."

"You are being foolish."

"Hear me out," Nate requested. "Kuruk is out to get *me*. His friends might lend a hand but only so long as he is there to lead them. If I can find them, if I can put an end to him, the rest will go. They won't pose a threat to you and your men."

"It's noble of you to be willing to risk your life on our behalf, but you're overlooking something."

"Which would be?"

"Kill Kuruk and maybe his friends won't go away. Maybe they will want revenge for him just as he wants revenge for his uncle. They might even send for more warriors, and before you know it, we'll have the whole tribe breathing down our necks. Have you considered that?"

No, Nate hadn't. "The risk is small. The Pawnees have never attacked whites in any great force."

"There's a first time for everything. But I won't try to stop you. You are a grown man and can do as you please. All I ask is that you don't go alone."

"You want me to take Haskell?"

"He is a fine lieutenant and has never given me cause to regret choosing him, but he's not the man for this job." Blunt twisted and scanned the encampment. Cupping his free hand to his mouth, he bellowed, "Maklin, a word with you, if you please."

The man who came to the fire was of middling height. He was dressed as the other bull-whackers except he wore a black hat with an uncommonly wide brim. He had two knives, one on each hip. Both of the pistols tucked on either side of his belt buckle were inlaid with silver. His rifle was foreign made, not a Hawken. He was the only freighter who wore moccasins and not boots.

Nate had seen the man around and noticed that he kept to himself and rarely spoke even to the other bull-whackers.

"Mr. Maklin, here, is from Texas. He lived for a while with the Lipans. Quick Hands, they called him. He is the best killer in my outfit and you would do well to have him at your side."

"You've lived with Apaches?" Nate had heard that they were implacable haters of all things white.

"I took a Lipan gal as my wife. She's dead now." Maklin didn't elaborate.

"We have something in common," Nate said. "My wife is Shoshone and her people adopted me. Did the Lipans adopt you?"

"I can go back to them anytime I want."

Blunt coughed. "I never pry into the past of my men except as it relates to their work, but I can assure you that you won't regret taking him."

Maklin turned to the captain. "What is it you want me to do?"

"You've heard about our guide's run-in with the Pawnees today? He intends to find their leader and kill him so the rest don't try to kill us."

Again Maklin asked, "What is it you want me to do?"

"Go with Mr. King. Watch his back. Protect him. Kill any Pawnees who try to kill him."

Nate smothered a chuckle. "I can take care of myself."

"Pride, sir, goes before a fall," Blunt responded. "Are you refusing Maklin's help?"

"Why do you call him the best killer you have?"

It was Maklin who answered. "Because I've killed

more than all the rest put together. Thirty-seven men, at last count. Some were white, but most were enemies of the Lipans."

"You keep a tally?"

"I don't take joy in spilling blood, if that's what you're thinking. It has to be done and I do it and forget it."

"Would that I could," Nate said half to himself. "All right. You can come along on one condition. You're not to kill unless I say. Do you agree?"

"He agrees," Blunt said.

Nate stood. "I'll go get ready." He made for the bay. As he crossed the circle he glanced back.

Jeremiah Blunt and the man called Maklin were huddled together, and Maklin was fingering one of his silver-inlaid pistols.

Chapter Six

No matter how small the fire, at night the glow could be seen for miles. Even when the fire was kindled in a hollow or a ravine as a precaution, a pale patch always stood out against the black ink of the night sky, especially when someone used a telescope to look for it as Nate was doing now. He sat astride the bay half a mile from the freighter camp and slowly swept the spyglass back and forth, seeking a telltale lighter patch.

"Anything?" Maklin asked.

"Not yet." Nate was convinced Kuruk was out there somewhere plotting to rub him out for the death of Red Rock.

"Ask you a question?"

"So long as it's not about anything personal."

"You say the Shoshones adopted you into their tribe. Did it mean something to you, or did you go along with it so as not to hurt their feelings?"

Nate lowered the spyglass and looked at him. "I like the Shoshones. They have my highest respect and I'm honored they've taken me as one of their own. Why do you ask?"

"A lot of whites don't care for Indians."

That was putting it mildly, Nate thought. Out loud he said, "A lot of people, white and red, can't see past the color of another person's skin."

"I can," Maklin said without a hint of brag. "I saw through that Lipan gal's skin to the beauty she had inside. I loved her, King. I loved her more than I've ever loved anything, a lot like you must love your Shoshone gal, I reckon."

Nate acknowledged as much.

"A lot of whites looked down their noses at me for taking her for my wife," Maklin detailed. "One day in a saloon a man called me a no-account, stinking Injun lover. His very words."

"What did you do?"

"I used the stock of my rifle on his face. I broke his nose and split his cheek. I told him if he ever pressed charges I'd come back and finish what I'd started. He never did."

"What was her name?"

"Na-lin. Yours?"

"Winona."

For a span of moments Nate felt a strong bond with this man he hardly knew. Then he raised the spyglass and applied it to the dark realm to the north. He was on his sixth sweep when his attention was drawn to a spot to the northeast.

"Something?" Maklin asked.

"Could be." Or it could be Nate's imagination, but there seemed to be the faintest of fire glows. "Here. Take a gander and see what you think." He pointed and gave the telescope to the Texan.

Maklin raised it to his right eye. He was still a bit, then said, "If it's them they're off a far piece."

Nate slid the spyglass into his parfleche and off they went. He held the bay to a walk, both for its own sake and for the fact that sound carried a long way at night and two horses at a trot or gallop made a lot of sound.

Maklin reverted to his usual laconic self and didn't say a word until more than half an hour later when he declared, "We're getting close."

Nate judged the fire to be a quarter of a mile off yet.

The pale patch had grown but not by much. He went on until he came on a stand of cottonwoods and willows. Dismounting, he led the bay in among them and tied the reins to a drooping willow branch. Shucking his Hawken from the sheath, he padded to the other side of the stand. The stretch of prairie beyond appeared flat, but in the dark appearances were always deceiving.

As silently as a specter, Maklin materialized. "Too bad the wind's not blowing from them to us."

"At least it's not blowing from us to them," Nate said. It was out of the northwest and blowing to the southeast and the glow was due east.

"You lead, I'll follow."

In a crouch Nate crept into the open. The high grass rustled against his legs but not loud enough to be heard more than a few feet away. Every dozen steps or so he raised his head. He had the glow pinpointed, but he couldn't see the fire. The reason became apparent when he came to a basin. Flattening, he crawled to the edge and peered over. To say he was surprised was an understatement.

Four people were below. They were white, not red, and judging by their shabby clothes and six swayback horses, they were not well off. A family, Nate reckoned. The father, a large husky with a big-boned frame, had a bushy beard and wore suspenders. The mother, her dress and bonnet faded homespun, was stirring a pot with a wooden spoon. The children were about ten or twelve, one a girl and the other a freckled boy, ragamuffins who stared at the pot as hungrily as starved wolves.

"The fools," Maklin whispered.

Nate stood and held the Hawken out from his side.

"Hail the fire!" he called down. "We are friendly and we'd like a word with you."

The four leaped to their feet. The girl and boy ran to the mother while the father picked up a rifle and stepped between his family and the rim, shielding his family with his body. "Who's that? Who's out there?"

"My name is Nate King. I am with some freighters who are camped to the south. May I come down?"

"So long as you do it nice and slow and keep your hands where I can see them."

Nate took a few steps and thought to add, "I have another man with me. Is it all right if we both descend?"

"The same applies to your friend."

Nate smiled to show he was friendly. He took in the sorry state of their effects and noted that their packs were tied with twine and not rope. Up close, he could see that the man's coat and the woman's dress had been patched many times over. "How do you do, folks?"

"Gosh," the boy said, peeking past his mother. "He looks almost Indian, Ma."

"Be polite," the woman cautioned.

"Well, he does."

"Quiet, Phillip," the father said sternly. He hadn't lowered his rifle. "What do you want, mister? If it's food, we'll share. But we don't have much."

"We already ate, thanks," Nate said. "I wanted to warn you. There are Pawnees in the area. It's not safe."

"I have this," the man said, wagging his rifle, "and I am a fair shot if I say so myself. Injuns don't worry me."

Maklin said, "They would if you had any sense."

"Here, now," the man bristled. "I won't be insulted. Who are you, anyhow? What do you know?"

"I know you are loco to be out here alone like this."

"We're on our way to Oregon. There's land to be had. Good land, fertile land. The crops practically grow themselves, folks say."

"You're a farmer," Nate guessed.

"Yes, sir. Wendell is my name. We hail from Missouri. Our county got so dry last year we lost our farm. In Oregon we aim to start over. I hear they never lack for rain."

"You'll never live to reach it," Maklin said.

Wendell took exception. "What a cruel thing to say, with my wife and young'ns standing right there."

Maklin turned to Nate. "Tell them. Make them see."

"Make us see what?" the farmer demanded.

Nate smiled at the mother and the children to try and put them at ease. "He's concerned for your family. You should be with a wagon train, not by yourselves."

"It costs money to sign on with a train," Wendell said. "It costs money for a wagon and money for a team and money for supplies, and money is one thing we are short of."

Nate could see that for himself. "You're taking a risk." Which was putting it mildly.

"You think I don't know that?" Wendell countered. "I'm not dumb. I talked it over with Maddy and she agreed we would cross the prairie as quick as we could and stick to cover once we're in the mountains. By sticking close to the Oregon Trail we should be in Oregon in five to six weeks."

Nate felt sorry for them. They thought they had it all worked out, but they were infants. "The Sioux, the Blackfeet, they know the routes the whites like to use."

"We're being careful," Wendell insisted, and motioned at the basin. "We made our fire where nobody can see, didn't we?"

"We saw it," Nate said.

"It's too late for us to turn back."

Nate knew that the dangers ahead were far worse than anything they had experienced so far. "Listen to me. Here's an idea. Join the freight train I'm with. Their captain won't mind. After I've guided them to where they want to go, I'll take you to a valley where my family and I live. You can stay with us, rest up a spell, and then we'll take you to the Oregon Trail and lend you the money to join a wagon train."

"We don't have a wagon," Maddy said.

"We'll ask the wagon master if you can ride with them anyway. Odds are he won't mind."

"You would do that?" Wendell asked.

Nate had more than enough in his poke at home. "I would do that."

"But you don't know me from Adam."

Maklin stepped past Nate. "What the hell is the matter with you? He's giving you a chance to go on breathing and you quibble?"

"Watch your tone," Wendell said.

The Texan pointed at the woman and children. "Think of them, damn you. Think of her after she's been raped and had her throat slit. Think of your boy and girl there after they've been cut to bits."

Wendell shook with fury. "How dare you talk to me like that? With my family right there. Who in hell do you think you are?" He started to jerk his rifle to his shoulder.

Maklin's hand flicked and a pistol was in it and pointed at Wendell, who froze in consternation. "Your temper is liable to get you killed someday, farmer. Set your long gun on the ground."

Reluctantly, Wendell tucked at the knees and carefully placed his rifle on the grass. As he unfurled he said, "I don't like you. I don't like you a whole lot."

"Forget about me. It's King, here, you should heed. Take him up on his offer or you'll live to regret it."

"I will do as I please," Wendell said.

Nate was as bewildered as the farmer. "Both of you need to calm down," he advised.

"I am perfectly calm," Maklin said. "I just can't stand to see this woman lose her life because her husband is too stupid to know when he's being dumb. They'll never make it to Oregon on their own. You know it and I know it and I wish to God they did." Suddenly stepping back, Maklin slid the pistol under his belt, wheeled, and melted into the darkness.

"Goodness gracious," Maddy breathed. "What on earth got into him?"

Nate was wondering the same thing. "I'll go have a talk with him. In the meantime, you two hash it over and decide." He turned partway. "He's right, though. On your own you're easy prey for every hostile who comes along. You would be a lot safer with the freighters." He walked up the slope and nearly tripped over Maklin, who had squatted on the rim. "What got into you down there?"

The Texan didn't answer.

"Why did you talk to him like that? It was bound to make him mad."

"He's a fool."

"He's doing what he can. We can't fault him for wanting a better life for his family."

"We can fault him for getting them killed, which he sure as hell will do unless he has more brains than I give him credit for."

Nate leaned on the Hawken. "There's more to it than that. I saw how you looked at that woman."

"I don't want her dead."

"What is she to you that you care so much? You just met her."

"She's noting to me. She's female, though, and females shouldn't have to go through that."

"Go through what?" Nate wished he could see Maklin's face, but it was hidden by the black hat's wide brim.

"What hostiles will do to her if they get their hands on her." Maklin bowed his head and said quietly, "I told you my wife is dead. I didn't tell you how she died."

Nate had an inkling and quickly said, "If you don't care to talk about it, that's fine."

"No. I want you to know. I want you to understand why that farmer made me so damn mad." Maklin's voice dropped lower. "The Comanches got hold of her, Nate. The Lipans and the Comanches have been enemies for as long as anyone can remember. They exterminate each other on sight."

"The Shoshones have their enemies, too." To Nate's knowledge all tribes did.

When it came to hate, the white and the red were more alike than either was willing to admit.

"Na-lin was off with four other women picking berries and they were taken by surprise. They ran, and one of the women hid in the bushes. She saw what happened." Maklin paused. "The Comanches caught Na-lin and the others. Na-lin fought them. She drew her knife and cut a warrior, so they threw her down and did things. . . ." Maklin stopped.

"No need to tell me more."

"I couldn't if I wanted to."

"Stay here. I'll be right back." Nate retraced his step to the bottom of the basin. They were waiting, the four of them, the father and mother with their arms around their children. "Have you decided?"

"Yes, we have," Wendell said. "We thank you for your offer, but we will continue on our own. It's not that we don't trust you—"

"But we don't know you," Maddy quickly explained.

"So we figure to keep going on our own," Wendell finished. He grinned and shrugged. "Heck, we've made it this far, we'll make it the rest of the way."

"God help you," Nate King said.

Chapter Seven

"Are those buzzards?" Jeremiah Blunt wondered.

Nate King had been deep in thought. He was thinking of Evelyn and the Nansusequa and hoping Shakespeare got them home safely. Now he glanced at the captain and then in the direction Blunt was staring and a chill rippled down his spine. To the northeast vultures were circling, an awful lot of them.

The freight wagons had been under way an hour and were strung out in single file.

Maklin rode on Nate's left. He had been with Nate since Nate woke up, at Blunt's orders, Nate suspected. Now the Texan swore and said, "That's about where we ran into that dirt farmer and his family."

"I'll catch up," Nate told Blunt, and brought the bay to a gallop. His shadow stayed with him. In due course they were close enough that Nate could see the bald heads and hooked beaks of the winged carrion eaters. He hoped against hope, but when he drew rein at the basin's rim, his hopes were dashed. "God, no."

"I hate idiots," Maklin said.

Nate gigged the bay down. A score of vultures rose into the air, flapping heavily, disturbed from their feast

The scent of so much fresh blood caused the bay to shy and snort. Nate had to calm it to get it to go all the way to the bottom. The gore, the viscera, the abominable things that had been done, churned his stomach. He came close to being violently sick.

"This wasn't no ordinary butchery," the Texan remarked.

Nate nodded, his mouth too dry to speak. The family had been tortured, tortured horribly, and then hacked and cut and chopped, even the little girl and boy.

Maklin asked the pertinent question. "Was it the Pawnees or someone else?"

Nate slid down. He tried to avoid stepping in the blood, but there was so much it was impossible. The killers had stepped in the blood, too, leaving footprints. He examined them.

No two tribes made their footwear the same way. A person would think that feet were feet, but each tribe had a distinct shape and stitch. Cheyenne moccasins were wider across the ball of the foot and tapered at the toes and the heel. Crow moccasins were a crescent. On Sioux moccasins the toes all curved inward. Pawnee moccasins were usually shorter than most others and narrowed from about the middle of the foot to the heel.

The footprints in the blood were short and narrowed from about the middle of the foot to the heel.

"Now we know," Maklin said.

Nate bowed his head. This was Kuruk's doing. He was as sure of it as he was of anything.

"He's rubbing your nose in his hate. Letting you know what he has in store for you."

Choked with emotion, Nate vowed, "Not if I kill him first."

The Texan nudged a severed finger with his toes. "This reminds me of what the Comanches did to Na-lin." He swore under his breath. "What kind of world is it that things like this can happen?"

Nate didn't have an answer. He had long since

stopped trying to figure it out. The best he could do, the best any man could do, was protect his loved ones as best he could from the cruelties life threw at him.

"Are you fixing to go after them?"

Nate considered. The freighters were on open prairie and had days of easy travel before they would reach South Pass. They didn't need him right now. "Your boss won't mind you tagging along?"

"He was the one who told me to stick to you like prickly pear." Maklin confirmed Nate's earlier hunch. "He doesn't want anything to happen to you."

"I told him I don't need a nursemaid."

"All I'm to do is watch your back."

"It might take a lot of watching."

Maklin motioned at the slaughter. "Do you want to bury them or leave them for the scavengers?"

"We'll do it on the way back." To Nate the important thing was to catch the culprits.

Their trail was plain enough. Eleven horses left a lot of tracks. They led to the north for over a mile and then off to the northeast.

Nate and Maklin went another mile and the Texan remarked, "Looks to me as if they're heading for Pawnee territory."

Nate thought so, too. Unless it was a ruse and Kuruk intended to circle back later.

"They're moving awful fast. It could take us days to catch them, if we ever do."

Nate came to a stop. Leaning on his saddle, he frowned.

"You're doing the right thing," Maklin said.

"By giving up?"

"By being smart. This smells of a trick. Could be this Kuruk aims to lure you into Pawnee territory."

Nate felt his jaw muscles twitch.

"It's not as if that dirt farmer and his family were kin of yours. As you reminded me last night, you only just met them."

"For a man who doesn't talk much, you have a leaky mouth."

Maklin grinned. "My boss says I'm to keep you alive. We keep on going and that might prove hard. Do we use our heads or do we lose them?"

"We turn back and bury what's left."

It was pushing sundown when they caught up with the freight wagons. Jeremiah Blunt took the news in grim spirit. "You did what you could. Their souls are in the Lord's hands now."

Nate blamed himself in part for the tragedy. Maybe if he had been more insistent, Wendell and his family would still be alive. But what else could he have done short of forcing them to join the freight train at the point of a gun?

By the next morning Nate had come to terms with his guilt. Blunt and Maklin were right; he *had* done all he could. Wendell and Maddy had brought it on themselves by not heeding his advice. The wilderness was a harsh mistress. She was cruel and merciless. Simpletons were fodder for her claws and fangs. The timid fell to her tomahawks and knives. Some people were too naive to see the thorns. Like Wendell, they relied on the hand of Providence or on luck to keep them alive. It never occurred to them that to a hungry grizzly or a hostile out to count coup, Providence didn't matter a lick. Luck was more fickle than the weather. To rely on chance when one's life was at stake was to have a secret death wish.

Day followed day without further incident. Nate got to know the freighters well.

On a sunny morning they started the climb to South

Pass, which wasn't much of a climb at all. When most easterners thought of a pass, they thought of a gap high on a mountain range. South Pass was the exception. The prairie rolled upward as gently as could be to the Continental Divide and then down the other side. To the north were the jagged peaks of the Wind River Range; to the south the land peaked to form the miles-high backbone of the Rockies.

South Pass was the one point where wagons could cross from one side of the Divide to the other with ease. Thousands of emigrants bound for Oregon and California had left the ruts of their passage. They had left other things, too. A stove, a grandfather clock, an anvil, tokens that even an easy climb had taxed teams pulling overburdened wagons.

Beyond lay a sage-sprinkled valley. The main trail bore to the southwest for a number of miles before it jagged to the northwest again and eventually brought travelers to Fort Hall.

Nate and the freighters left the trail shortly after South Pass, making for the rugged mountains to the north. From that point on, the freighters relied on Nate to guide them. Few whites had ever ventured into the geyser country. The tales of steaming springs and spouts of hot water hundreds of feet high had brought the region the label of "hell on earth." No one ever went there, which had Nate wondering about the Shakers.

Nate had been to the area twice. Both times he had taken the same route, north up Bridger Basin and then along the Green River to where it flowed down out of the Green River Range. From there on it was solid mountain travel.

Nate chose a different route this time. He had them cross a low unnamed range and follow a long, winding valley to the banks of the Gros Ventre River. By paralleling it they didn't want for water or graze, and while now and then the men had to wield axes to clear the way, the going was easier than on the slopes above.

The oxen were unflagging, but their progress, through no fault of theirs, was slow.

The mountains were magnificent. Peaks that towered almost three miles into the sky. Slopes forested thick with spruce and fir and stands of shimmering aspens. Meadows that ran riot with the colors of wildflowers.

Wildlife was everywhere. Black-tailed deer raised their tails in alarm and bounded off. Elk hid in the deep thickets. Bear sign told of black bears and grizzlies. Eagles ruled the air. Hawks dived for prey. Ravens squawked and flapped. Squirrels in the trees and squirrels on the ground scampered and chattered. Songbirds warbled an avian orchestra.

They were now deep in the heart of the Gros Ventre Range. To the northwest were the Tetons. Beyond, the spectacular geyser country. The Valley of Lost Skulls was at its southernmost edge.

Another ten days brought them to where Nate felt they could come on the valley at any time. As he told Jeremiah Blunt, he'd never been there, but based on what Shakespeare had told him and other accounts, the landmarks were right. It should be near.

As added proof, the country changed. The mountain slopes were not as thickly forested. Lower down, where vegetation usually thrived, the little that grew was stunted and withered, as if the plants were being poisoned by the ground. Deer became scarce. There was no bear sign. Eagles and hawks disappeared from the sky. Ravens were never seen. Nor squirrels or rabbits or any of the small game formerly so abundant.

The birds fell silent. Not a single, solitary note broke the disquieting stillness.

Nate could understand why it gave people the jitters. The silence, the twisted shapes of the rocks, the absence of life, gnawed at the nerves. Bad medicine the Indians called it, and they were right.

He roved on ahead of the wagons to try and locate the valley. As usual, the Texan accompanied him. The shod hooves of their mounts sounded like hammers on the rock.

A reek filled the air, a foul stench explained when they came on a pool of bubbling water no bigger around than a washtub.

The Texan coughed and said, "So this is what hell smells like?"

They rode on. It was a maze, this country, and Nate began to think he had been overconfident and the Valley of Skulls would be a lot harder to find than he imagined when they came on ruts. Wagons, a lot of wagons, had come in from the east. It had to be the Shakers, Nate reckoned. No other wagon train that he knew of had ever penetrated this far.

"These people must be crazy," Maklin remarked.

Nate wondered, too.

The tracks led to the northwest along a ribbon of a stream that had no name. It had another quality, which Nate discovered by accident when he dipped his hand in the water to drink. "It's warm."

"What?" Maklin said.

"This water. It's warm enough to use for bathwater."

The Texan climbed down to see for himself. "I'll be damned. Is it safe to drink, you reckon?"

Nate dared a sip. Save for a slight metallic taste, the sip produced no ill effects.

"I wouldn't want to drink this regular," was Maklin's assessment.

Neither would Nate. They climbed back on their mounts. The wagon tracks hugged the stream and they did the same until along about the middle of the afternoon when it brought them to a narrow cleft dark with shadow. There was barely enough room for a wagon to pass through.

Nate entered the cleft. He didn't like being hemmed by rock and was glad when after only thirty feet they emerged to have a valley floor spread out before them. Not a valley of grass and flowers but a valley of rock and boulders. Grotesque stone shapes testified to a geologic upheaval in the remote past that had bent and twisted the foundations of the earth.

Both abruptly drew rein.

"Is that *singing*?" Maklin asked in amazement.

Nate heard it, too, wafting from deeper in the valley, around a bend that hid what lay beyond. "They don't even post a guard," he noted. Then again, what need did they have of a sentry when the Indians wouldn't come anywhere near the place?

They rode around the bend and again drew rein.

"Pinch me so I know I'm not dreaming," Maklin said.

The valley broadened. To the north and south it was rimmed by high ramparts pockmarked with the dark openings to caves. The ground was rock, dark rock dotted with pale patches, broken here and there by pools that bubbled and hissed and gave off steam. Ahead, perhaps half a mile, grew an area of green, and there, parked in rows, were Conestogas. A corral held horses and mules. Two buildings had been built, long and low and made of logs, and a third was being erected. Around and among the buildings and wagons moved dozens of people, many singing as they worked.

"We should introduce ourselves and tell them their supplies will be here soon," Nate proposed. He raised his reins and was about to move on when his gaze alighted on what he had taken for pale rock.

"A skull!" Maklin exclaimed.

That it was, far bigger than the skull of any grizzly or buffalo. Others were scattered here and there, along with giant spine bones and legs bones and even rib bones. But the skulls far outnumbered the rest. Strange skulls. Unnatural skulls. Skulls of creatures from another time.

Nate passed one with three horns, two of which were broken. Another skull was ringed by teeth as long as his fingers.

"What monsters were these?" the Texan marveled.

Then, around a boulder, skipped a young woman in her twenties wearing a pretty yellow dress. Around her throat was a neckerchief and on her head she wore a small cap. She was carrying a basket, and on seeing them she flashed a friendly smile. "How do you do, kind sirs? On behalf of my brethren, I bid you welcome to Second Eden."

Chapter Eight

The Shakers were well dressed, the women in bright dresses and all wearing neckerchiefs and the same type of cap. The men wore jackets and trousers and short-brimmed hats. Oddly, all the men wore their hair the same way: long at the back, cut in bangs at the front. They constantly smiled and many sang hymns of praise as they bustled about. The arrival of Nate and Maklin barely caused a stir. Curious glances were thrown their way, but no one stopped his or her work to come over and ask who they were and what they were doing there.

The young woman with the basket ushered them past the wagons and the corral and the two completed log buildings to where a third structure was being erected. The men did the actual building. The women were involved with other tasks.

Nate noticed that they were equally divided between the sexes. All were grown men and grown women. There wasn't a child to be seen. That struck him as peculiar. So did the fact that while the Shakers smiled and sang as they worked, none stood around talking. He nodded at a gray-haired woman who smiled at him and again at a man who had paused in sawing a log to mop his sweaty brow.

"They remind me of a bunch of bees," Maklin said.

The young woman overheard. "I thank you for the compliment. Elder Lexington says we must keep as busy as bees if we are to have our buildings done and our provisions stocked for the coming winter."

"At least they have the brains to do that," Maklin said to Nate.

Most people would be offended by the comment but not the young woman. She laughed and said, "Oh yes, sir. Elder Lexington is very smart. He's the smartest man I know. Why, he can quote the entire Bible by heart. And look, here he is now."

From around the nearest log building came a middle-aged man on the portly side with a middle-aged woman of the same stout build. They gazed about—as might overseers on a plantation, only overseers with benign smiles and the serene air of earthbound angels. The young woman beckoned and the pair walked over.

"Who have you here, Sister Benedine?" the man asked.

"Outsiders, Elder Lexington. They say they are with the man you hired to bring our supplies." The young woman pointed. "This is Brother King and Brother Maklin."

The Texan said gruffly, "I'm not your brother, girl, or anyone else's."

"But that you are," Lexington said. "Surely you have heard that in the eyes of the Lord we are all brothers and sisters, and he who loveth God must love his brother also?"

"Where was this God of yours when my Na-lin was being gutted like a fish?" Maklin snapped.

"I beg your pardon?"

Maklin turned to Nate. "They raise my hackles. I'll be over by that pool yonder if you need me." So saying, he gigged his mount toward the stream.

"My word," Lexington said. "I didn't mean to upset him so. Whatever is the matter?"

"Don't fret yourself, Brother," said the stout woman beside him. "He is an outsider. Outsiders have no true conception."

Lexington looked up at Nate. "How about you, Brother King? Do we raise your hackles as well?"

Nate did feel uncomfortable, but he couldn't explain why. "You have to excuse him. His wife was butchered by the Comanches."

"Ah, well," Lexington said sympathetically.

"The Lord works in mysterious ways," the stout woman said. "Your friend would be better served if he were to realize that all things work to the glory of God."

Nate couldn't see how in this instance, but he held his tongue and said, "If you don't mind, I'll collect him and we'll head back. If we push the wagons, Blunt can be here by tomorrow evening."

"But you just got here," Lexington said. "Why not rest a bit and I will give you a tour?"

"Pride, Brother," the woman said.

"I know, Sister Amelia, but they are our first visitors. And who knows, Brother King, here, might take it into his head to become a member of Second Eden."

"That's what you call this place?"

"I picked the name myself," Elder Lexington confirmed. "Frankly, I can't think of a more fitting name."

Nate gazed at the stark rocky ramparts speckled by the dark mouths of caves and the valley floor littered with gleaming skulls and dotted by bubbling hot springs, boiling mud pots, and hissing steam vents. "I can think of one."

Arthur Lexington chuckled. "I can guess what it is, too. In a year, though, we will have transformed this valley into the Eden we would like it to be. You wait and see."

"Amen," Sister Amelia said. She turned to the younger woman. "You can go now, Sister Benedine. Pick a basketful of flowers and be back here within the hour."

"I will, Sister," Benedine said, and cheerfully headed back down the valley, swinging her basket and humming.

Alarm spiked Nate into saying. "Did I hear that right? She's going out of the valley to get flowers?"

"There are none in Second Eden as yet, Brother King," Lexington said. "That will change once we cultivate the soil."

Nate was going to ask how they would go about cultivating rock since that was what most of the valley consisted of, but he had a weightier concern. "It's not safe."

"What isn't?" Sister Amelia asked.

"Sending that girl out alone. She could run into hostiles or a mountain lion or you name it."

"Pshaw," Amelia scoffed. "She'll be perfectly fine. The Lord will watch over her and protect her."

Nate thought of Wendell and his family and what was left of them at the bottom of the basin. "Send someone with her. Someone with a gun."

Elder Lexington and Sister Amelia looked at each other and then at Nate, and smiled those benign smiles.

"You must know very little about the Shakers, Brother King," Lexington said. "We do not believe in violence. We do not believe in killing. There isn't a single gun in this valley except for yours and Brother Maklin's."

"*What?*" Nate was shocked to his core. "You came

all this way, clear across the prairie and into these mountains, without any way to protect yourselves?"

"The Lord is our buckler and our shield," Lexington intoned. "He safeguards us from harm."

"Dear God."

"I'll thank you not to take the Lord's name in vain, Brother King," Sister Amelia said sternly.

"You don't understand," Nate said, bending down. "That girl could be killed. All of you could. That you made it this far and lasted this long is a miracle."

"Exactly," Lexington said, and beamed. "Added proof that the Almighty is indeed watching over us as He does the lowly sparrow."

Nate glanced over his shoulder. Sister Benedine was past the corral. "Please. Send a man along."

"Oh, that wouldn't do," Sister Amelia said. "That wouldn't do at all."

"I should say not," Elder Lexington agreed. "You must be more observant, Brother King. "Or haven't you noticed that the men and women in our colony do not work side by side?"

"We do not believe in mingling," Amelia elaborated. "Males and females do not work together. They do not eat together. They certainly do not share the same sleeping quarters."

"Why not?"

Lexington chuckled at Amelia. "He certainly doesn't know anything about us, does he? Perhaps I should enlighten him." He crooked a finger. "Come with us, Brother King, if you would."

Nate dismounted and gazed after Sister Benedine, who was still skipping along. Frowning, he followed the leader of the colony and Sister Amelia over to the building under construction.

"You will note that only men do the building," Elder

Lexington pointed out. "The women are busy with washing clothes and sewing and preparing food."

"Each gender has its own sphere," Amelia said.

Nate shrugged. "That's not much different from the outside world." Not that he entirely approved. There were many things women could do as well as men but were looked down on if they did.

"True," Lexington conceded. "But the Shakers take it a step further." He paused and gave an odd sort of grin. "I trust you are familiar with our philosophy toward procreation?"

"What?" Nate had been looking down the valley again. Sister Benedine was almost out of sight.

"Our attitude toward having children, and toward— pardon me, Sister Amelia for being vulgar—the act that produces them."

Nate kept quiet. He was fond of that act, himself.

"Shakers never, ever give sway to their carnal natures. We suppress them. We smother them. We eliminate them from our lives. We don't give them a chance to enter our heads."

Nate didn't see how that was possible, but again he kept silent.

"In our communities east of the Mississippi," Elder Lexington continued, "men and women are always separated. They sleep in separate rooms. They enter and leave buildings through separate doors. When they must meet for meals or what have you, they sit on opposite sides of the room."

"Only when we worship do we mingle," Sister Amelia declared. "For then the hand of the Lord is upon us."

"Exactly," Lexington agreed. "As you may see for yourself before your stay with us is concluded." He pointed at the two long, low log structures. "Do you see those? We have taken the separation a step more.

One of those buildings is for the men, the other for the women."

"We believe in as near complete separation as possible," Sister Amelia explained. "It is one of Elder Lexington's views that caused us to break away from the main movement and start our own colony."

Elder Lexington raised an ecstatic face to the heavens. "We must be pure for our Maker, Brother King. We must be ready at all times for the advent of the Second Coming."

Nate finally had to say something. "But if you don't have children, who will carry on after you're gone?"

Lexington turned and put a hand on Nate's shoulder. "We grow by converting others, Brother King."

"Back in the States they also adopt children, but that is another thing Brother Lexington is against," Sister Amelia revealed.

Lexington clucked like an irate hen. "Our brothers and sisters descend on orphanages and take away ten or twenty at a time. Their intentions are praiseworthy, but I think it wrong. Children are incapable of appreciating God to the fullest. They can't enter heaven because they are flawed."

Nate could only stare.

"Ah. I see that look," Lexington said. "But I know whereof I speak. I have seen the truth in a vision."

"A vision," Sister Amelia echoed.

Nate gazed about him. The smiling faces, the singing, the hustle and bustle: he began to see them in a different light. "I could never be a Shaker."

"Never say never," Elder Lexington said with a smirk. "But why not, may I ask?"

Nate looked him in the eye. "I have a son and a daughter. I love them dearly. They're not perfect. None of us are. But they aren't flawed, either. Not in the way you mean."

"Now, Brother King, don't misconstrue. I'm not saying children are evil, although as the fruit of our loins they bear the taint of sin. I am merely saying they are incomplete. They can't experience God to His fullness."

"All Shakers think that?"

"Oh no, or else those back East wouldn't adopt as they do. But it's why we didn't bring any children with us."

Nate gazed about him again at the dark cave mouths and the mostly rock valley floor and the bubbling cauldrons, and was glad they hadn't. "Can I ask you a question?"

"Anything, Brother, anything at all."

"Why did you come *here* of all places? Why come to this godforsaken valley when there are so many better spots?"

"Better?" Elder Lexington said, and chuckled. "You will understand better when—" He suddenly stopped and glanced down. "Do you feel it?" he asked excitedly. "Do you feel the power of the Lord?"

What Nate felt was a slight shaking under his feet. The very ground was trembling, as a man might when he was cold. It lasted only a few seconds and stopped.

Clasping his hands, Arthur Lexington cried to the sky in rapture, "Thank you, Lord, for that sign! Thank for you answering Brother King and showing him the truth."

"You think God caused that?" Nate asked in amazement.

"Of course. God causes all." Lexington closed his eyes and his smile widened. "When I first heard of this place, I knew it was a sign. I prayed and I prayed and I had a vision. In it I saw a new colony. More than a colony, really. I saw a new city, a great shining city of brethren in the United Society of Believers in Christ's Second Appearing. Thousands of us, many thousands, living as beacons to the rest of the world."

"Praise you, Elder Lexington," Sister Amelia said.

"Can you imagine, Brother King? The clean of heart, the very purest of the pure, letting their light so shine that God will look down from on high and be greatly pleased."

Nate was about to ask how Lexington could speak for the Almighty when from down the valley, faint but unmistakable, came a piercing scream.

Chapter Nine

The clatter of the bay's hooves on rock was like the beat of hammers.

Nate swept out of the valley and promptly drew rein. He glanced right and left but saw no sign of Sister Benedine. The scream had been her only outcry, and he was unsure which way she had gone. Then he spied her basket lying at the edge of the forest and he used his heels on the bay.

Scarlet drops spattered the basket and the grass. Fresh, glistening, dripping, the start of a trail of red that led into the trees.

Nate had his Hawken in his left hand. He rode slowly, cautiously. He had yet to determine who or what had attacked her.

Another dozen strides of the bay and Nate had his answer. He stopped and stared down in horror at the print clearly outlined in a plate-sized ring of blood. The shape, the size, the length of the claws. "Griz," he said aloud.

The bay snorted and whinnied and stamped. It didn't like the blood. It didn't like the scent of the grizzly, either.

"Easy, boy," Nate said, and patted its neck.

The thud of hooves, the crackle of brush, and Maklin was next to him. The Texan took one look at the print, and swore. "I heard the girl and saw you light out." He raised his rifle. "She's dead by now. You know that, don't you?"

Nate nodded, and rode on. Every nerve in his body jangled with dread. He had tangled with enough grizzlies to be all too aware of how unpredictable they were, and how deadly. When aroused, they were savagery incarnate and virtually unstoppable.

"Those idiot Shakers are coming, but a fat lot of good they'll be. You can't fight a griz with love."

"Quiet," Nate said. He was straining his ears for the slightest sound. For all their bulk, grizzlies could be as silent as ghosts when they wanted to be, and it wouldn't surprise him if this particular griz had heard them and was waiting to charge.

From somewhere up ahead came a crunch, as of teeth on bone.

The bay stopped and stamped. Nate quickly slid down and thrust the reins at Maklin. "Stay here," he whispered, and advanced alone. He made less noise and with luck could take the bear by surprise.

The crunching grew louder.

Nate shuddered to think what was happening. Steeling himself, he crept past several spruce to a shoulder-high boulder. He crouched and edged far enough around to see a clearing on the other side—and what was in the middle of the clearing. His stomach did a flip-flop and bile rose in his gorge.

Typical of its kind, the grizzly was huge. Monstrous with muscle and bristling with hair, with a huge blunt head and a maw rimmed with razor daggers, it was chewing on a leg. Just a leg; it had ripped the limb off Sister Benedine and was feasting on the flesh.

The bear's back was to Nate. He didn't have a clear shot. Nor could he see Sister Benedine. Staying low, he began to circle. A few steps and he saw her.

The young Shaker lay on her side, her arms and remaining leg akimbo. Her cap was missing. Her dress was slashed and bloody and part of it, and parts of her, had been torn away. A crimson pool was forming under her; her cheek lay in her blood. Her eyes were wide.

Nate thought she was dead. Then she blinked, and moved. She was alive—and she was looking right at him.

"Please," she said.

The bear growled and raised its red-rimmed mouth from her leg.

"Please," she said again.

Nate knew what she wanted. He knew the risk it would put him in. He knew, too, what it would do to him, the nightmares it would bring. She wouldn't survive what the bear had done; she was suffering terribly and would endure worse when the bear turned from her leg to devour the rest of her.

Nate raised the Hawken. He thumbed back the hammer. He pulled on the rear trigger to set the front trigger and curled his finger around the front trigger.

Sister Benedine did the last thing he expected. She smiled and said with tears in her eyes, "Thank you."

At the blast the grizzly wheeled around and roared. Instantly, Nate clawed for a pistol. His were .55-caliber smoothbores. At this range they were almost as effective as a rifle. He swept one up and out and thumbed back the hammer, bracing for the bear's rush and the onslaught of fang and claw.

Only the bear wasn't there. The grizzly had spun back again and was halfway across the clearing. Bellowing at the top of its lungs, it plunged into the vegetation on the other side and crashed off into the woods, raising a racket that sent birds winging in panicked flight and squirrels scampering in fear to the tops of trees.

Nate waited, every sinew tense. He refused to accept the griz was gone. It would circle and attack. The seconds stretched into a minute and the minute stretched into several, and the bear didn't appear. "I'll be switched," he said. Luck had favored him. The bear had been rattled by the shot and the smoke.

Nate moved into the open. Sister Benedine's leg lay a few feet away, chunks missing from the thigh. As for Benedine herself, her eyes were still wide, but they were glazing over. "You asked an awful lot of me," Nate sadly told the body.

With barely any sound at all, Maklin was there. He stood over Sister Benedine and said simply, "Hell."

"She asked me to," Nate said softly.

"You did right. That bear would've ripped her to bits. You spared her a lot of pain and suffering."

Nate stooped and gently closed her eyes. "I'll fetch a blanket and we'll wrap her in it and bury her." He turned as the undergrowth crackled anew. Into the clearing burst Elder Lexington and Sister Amelia and others. They showed little emotion as they ringed the ghastly corpse.

"Poor Sister Benedine," Lexington said. "Taken from us when she was so young and so vibrant with the love of the Lord."

"It was God's will," another Shaker said.

"His works He performs in mysterious ways," remarked another.

Maklin swore and jabbed a finger at Lexington. "*You're* the one they should blame. You're the one who dragged these people out here. If you hadn't gotten your harebrained notion, that girl would still be breathing."

"It was the Lord's idea for us to come here, not mine."

Maklin nodded at the girl's remains. "The Lord should be right pleased with Himself."

Sister Amelia swung toward him. "This makes twice now you've taken our Maker's name in vain. I won't have it again, do you hear?"

"Be at peace, Sister," Lexington said.

"I can't help it, Elder. He has no faith, this one. He slanders us and he slanders He who made us."

"How about you, Brother King?" Lexington asked. "Do you blame us for Sister Benedine's death as well?"

"You should have sent someone with her," was all Nate said.

"If I had, we would have two bodies to bury." Lexington raised his arms to his followers. "Heed me. Brother Simon, you and Brother Bartholomew build a coffin. Keep it plain. Use pine and pitch. Sister Barclay, we'll need refreshments. Sister Amelia, spread the word that we will conduct the service right after the sun goes down."

"You're holding a funeral?" Maklin said.

"Oh, goodness, no. We celebrate life, not death. Our service is a loving testament to Sister Benedine. We are committing her spirit to the care of the Lord. Both of you are invited."

"No, thanks," Nate said. "We should get back. Jeremiah Blunt is waiting to hear if we've found the Valley of Skulls."

Lexington grinned and wagged a finger at him. "Ah, ah. The Valley of Skulls is no more. We call it Second Eden now, remember?"

"Calling a hog a cow doesn't mean it will moo," Maklin said.

"How is that again?"

Maklin turned to Nate. "Let's get the hell out of

here. Another minute of these lunkheads and I'll bust a vein." He lashed his reins and trotted off.

"What on earth is the matter with him?" Sister Amelia asked. "He has acted bitter toward us from the moment we met."

"I don't rightly know," Nate said, and lifted his reins. "I should catch up. Nice meeting you."

"Go with God," Lexington said.

Maklin had slowed and was scowling at the world and everything in it. He glanced around as Nate came up but didn't say anything.

"Well?"

"Well, what?" Maklin growled.

"What was that all about?"

"I told you. Do-goods like them raise my hackles. They go around with blinders on and want the rest of us to do the same."

"That's all there is to it?"

"What more do you need?" the Texan retorted. "Damn it. You saw how they are. Smiling all the time. Prattling on about how we're all brothers and sisters and the rest of that hogwash."

"That's cause to hate them?"

"I hate stupid, and they are as stupid as hell. The first war party that finds them will put an end to them right quick."

Nate had to agree. He told the Texan about their detest for weapons.

"There. See? Not one damn gun, they said? If that isn't stupid I don't know what is."

Nate mentioned that Maklin had acted the same way toward Wendell and his family.

"So? That dirt farmer was just as stupid. He deserved to be rubbed out just as these Shakers do."

"No one *deserves* to die," Nate disagreed, and rubbed his chin. "Did you feel this way before Na-lin was killed?"

"Maybe I did and maybe I didn't. I don't recollect."

In a flash of insight, Nate saw the truth. "You're not fooling anyone. At least not me."

"What's that supposed to mean?"

Nate didn't answer.

"If you think I care, you're wrong. I don't care about anyone anymore. Not after Na-lin." Maklin pulled his hat brim lower. "That's when I learned my lesson. That's when I realized how wrong I was. I used to believe, yes. I used to think just like Wendell and Lexington. Oh, I didn't go around quoting Scripture or praying every damn day, but I believed there was a God and there was a purpose to all of this." Maklin shook his head. "Not anymore. Now I know better."

Nate thought of Winona and how he would feel if anything were to happen to her.

"You saw that dirt farmer. You saw what the Pawnees did to his wife and his kids. Look me in the eye and tell me there's a God of love somewhere that watches over people. Look me in the eye and tell me something like that makes sense to you."

"I . . ." Nate began, and stopped.

"I didn't think so. Where's the love in a woman having her intestines cut out? Where's the love in a little girl having her nose and her ears hacked off? Where's the love in a grizzly tearing the leg off someone?"

"I don't have all the answers."

"Hell, if you're like me, you don't have any." Maklin glowered at the sky. "I take that back. There's one answer I have. The answer to the biggest question of all." He paused. "There's no God. There never was. There never will be. We made God up. We had to. Otherwise the intestines and the noses and ears and legs would drive us insane."

"I think you're wrong," Nate said. "I can't prove it, but there has to be more to all this."

"More how? That if we die and go to heaven it makes all the rest of it right?" Maklin shook his head. "No. I refuse to be fooled. You want to believe, go ahead. But I'm telling you. If you're right and I'm wrong, if there really is a God, then either God doesn't give a damn about us or He's plumb loco."

On that they lapsed into silence.

The wagon train had covered a lot of ground since they left. Jeremiah Blunt was happy to hear they had found the Valley of Skulls, but he wasn't happy about the rest of their news.

"I was afraid of this," the captain said gravely. "When Arthur Lexington looked me up in St. Louis to hire me to deliver supplies, I tried to talk him out of his venture. I warned him that it was entirely possible he would get himself and his followers killed."

"How did he take it?" Nate asked.

Blunt colored pink. "He told me that if I was as devout as I claim to be, I'd have more trust in the Lord."

"I need a drink," Maklin said, and walked off.

"Remember my rule," Blunt said after him. "Not on the trail. Whiskey and work don't mix." He turned to Nate. "So tell me. This Pawnee who blames you for his uncle's death. Kuruk, isn't it? He speaks English, does he?"

"As well as you or me. Other languages, besides."

"Where did he learn them?"

"From a missionary, I think. Other whites have visited them, too. Major Long. Zebulon Pike. They've had a lot of contact with whites."

"Didn't the Pawnees send a delegation to meet with the president in Washington?"

"President Jefferson, yes."

"Do you suppose this Kuruk can write as well as read?"

Nate shrugged. "I wouldn't know. Why are you bringing all this up?"

"While you were gone, our wrangler was killed and some of our horses were run off," Blunt revealed. "Come with me. I have something to show you."

The body was in the last wagon, wrapped in a tarp. Blunt had it hauled out and set at Nate's feet and unwrapped the tarp himself. "Notice anything?"

Carved into the dead man's forehead were the letters *NK*.

Chapter Ten

There had been no sign of the Pawnees, Blunt told Nate. The wrangler was found dead shortly after Nate and Maklin left to scout for the Valley of Skulls. Blunt ended with "You know what that might mean, don't you?"

A chill ran through Nate. He was on the bay and ready to ride out in minutes. "Maklin can guide you to the valley. I'll wait there for you."

"You'll be riding in the dark."

"Can't be helped," Nate said, and bobbed his chin at the last wagon. "I won't be to blame for more."

"Noble of you," Jeremiah Blunt said, and offered his hand. "I can spare two or three men to go along."

"I'll travel faster alone. Besides, you might need them there." Nate had dallied long enough. With a slap of his legs he was off. The bay had not had much rest, but he pushed, riding at a trot when he could and only allowing the bay brief rests. He was thinking of the Shakers, those helpless, defenseless Shakers, and what a Pawnee war party would do to them.

Nate wanted to kick himself. If anything happened to the Shakers, their fate fell squarely on his shoulders.

The sun sank below the western horizon in a blaze of pink and yellow and red. Nate rode in near pitch-black. There was no moon, only starlight to ride by, and in the woods and gorges most was blocked out. He had to slow or risk losing the bay to a broken leg.

Nate mused on his encounter with the Pawnees all

those years ago. He had been lucky to get out of their village alive. He never expected this to happen, to have his past endanger his present. He was glad Winona wasn't along, or her life would be in peril, too.

The night dragged. The thud of the bay's heavy hooves punctuated the haunting howls of wolves and the high-pitched yips of coyotes. From time to time a roar or a screech broke the stillness. So, too, did the cries of prey: bleats, screams, even shrieks.

Nate remembered how it was growing up in New York, remembered visits to an uncle's farm bordered by forest, and how the night was seldom pierced by bestial sounds. In part, he reckoned, because a lot of the game had been killed off. In part, too, because the presence of man made the animals wary. When they were hunted day in and night out, stealth and silence became their way of life.

Another roar echoed off the high peaks.

Here, life was different. Here, the animals lived much as they had before the advent of man. The wilderness was as wilderness was meant to be: wild, untamed, savage.

Woe to the unwary, to those like the Shakers who came into the wilds like babes into the world, filled with trust and peace and convinced the rest of the world was as they were. Maklin was right about them having blinders on.

It was well past midnight when Nate neared the Valley of Skulls. Twice he heard grunts that might be the same griz that killed Sister Benedine, but they were off in the brush. At the valley mouth he drew rein and tested the night with his senses.

Once around the bend Nate drew rein again. The valley was completely dark. Not one of the windows glowed with the light from a lamp or candle. He imagined—he hoped—they had doused the lights when they turned in, and there wasn't a more sinister explanation.

An eerie feeling came over Nate as he rode amid the littered bones of bygone creatures while above reared the heights pockmarked with caves. He would like to explore those caves sometime soon. Who knew what he might find?

A bubbling sound reminded Nate of the hot springs. There was a hiss, and he flinched when hot drops spattered him. The bay nickered. Quickly, he reined away from the pool.

The Shakers were asking for misery by staying there. Somehow, Nate must convince them to go back East or else pick a more habitable spot.

The hoot of an owl from somewhere above was followed by a cry such as Nate had never heard, a wavering moan that might have come from out of one of the caves, a moan so human it made Nate think of a soul in torment. Involuntarily, he shuddered.

A gust of wind brought with it a whiff of a foul odor, sulfurous and vile. Nate almost gagged. He had not smelled anything like it when he was there earlier.

Suddenly Nate drew rein. High up at the caves a pale shape had appeared. It seemed to roil and writhe as if alive, yet it was as formless as fog. It was there and then with another gust of wind it was gone. He didn't know what to make of it.

Presently, Nate reached the corral. He stripped the bay, draped his saddle and saddle blanket over the top rail, and put the bay in with the other horses. Rather than knock on a door and wake the Shakers, he went to the Conestogas and climbed into the first one he came to. It was empty. The bed was hard but comfortable enough and he was out of the wind and night chill.

Curling onto his side, Nate willed his body to relax. A strange sense of forboding gripped him, a sense that he shouldn't be there, that he should flee while he could. It was silly, he told himself. Those stories about the valley had frayed his nerves.

Still, the Indians said the valley was bad medicine, and the Indians should know. It had been Nate's experience that their legends were steeped in truth. Maybe the facts had been twisted in the many retellings, but if they said the valley was bad medicine, then by God, it was.

With that troubling thought, Nate drifted off. He slept fitfully. A loud hiss awakened him once. Another time, it was a slight shake of the wagon. The ground was quaking again. The tremor only lasted ten seconds, but it was unnerving just the same.

Dawn had not yet creased the sky with the glow of the rising sun when Nate climbed from the wagon, and stretched. He was stiff and sore and famished.

The patch of green at the valley's heart covered about ten acres. Already the Shakers had chopped down a third or more of the trees to build their cabins and the corral. Nate gathered an armful of limbs and got a fire going near the corral. He put coffee on to perk and hunkered close to the flames for the warmth.

Leather hinges creaked, and a figure emerged from the building reserved for the men.

"You're up early," Nate said.

Arthur Lexington wore his beatific smile and carried a large Bible. "I am always the first up." He gazed across the valley as a baron might over his domain. "I'm surprised to find you back so soon. I thought you were coming with the wagons."

"There's a complication," Nate said, and told him about the Pawnees and the dead farmer and the dead wrangler.

"Ah. You came ahead because you feared for our safety? I thank you for your concern, but you needn't worry about us. The Lord will watch over us and deliver us from harm."

"Tell that to Sister Benedine."

Lexington's smile widened. "I assure you that her soul is in Paradise even as we speak." He paused. "Do you like us, Brother King?"

"Like has nothing to do with it. I don't understand you," Nate confessed. "I don't savvy why you chose *here*, of all places, to settle."

"Ah," Lexington said again. "Perhaps all will be made clear if you attend our evening gathering."

Just then the ground shook. Nate gave a start and reached for the coffeepot to steady it.

"Isn't it glorious?" Lexington said.

"Doesn't it worry you just a little?"

"Why should it? This valley has been here for ages, I understand. Those high walls, that stream, are unchanged from the dawn of time." Lexington chuckled. "The tremors are nothing to be afraid of. Quite the contrary. They speak to the glory of God."

"You've lost me."

"You'll understand this evening, I promise you," Lexington assured him. "You and the freighters are to be our guests."

Once the sun was up, Nate searched outside the valley for sign of the Pawnees. He found none, but that only meant Kuruk was being clever. The Pawnees were around somewhere, watching and waiting for the right moment to strike.

By the time Nate returned, the Shakers were once again bustling like bees, human bees that hummed and sang and smiled. The men chopped trees, hewed logs, and worked on the third building. The women washed clothes in the stream or skinned potatoes for the cooking pot or worked on quilts.

Despite the incident with the bear and Nate's warning about the war party, no sentries were posted.

Nate needed to talk to Lexington but couldn't find him. He spied Sister Amelia by the corral and asked to see him.

"Elder Lexington is in the men's quarters," Amelia said, with a bob of her double chin at the log dwelling.

"Will you take me to him?"

Amelia's eyebrows rose. "Haven't you been paying attention, Brother King? In our society men and women never mingle except when they must. I am no more permitted to go into their living quarters than they are to enter our living quarters."

"Do you like it that way?"

"What a silly question," Amelia said. "I wouldn't be a Shaker if I didn't." She glanced over at the men sweating and toiling, and sniffed. "To be honest, I have never felt comfortable around men. You are peculiar creatures, every one of you."

"Some ladies like us."

"Don't be flippant. Ideally, God would never have separated us to begin with unless it was meant to be."

"Care to explain?"

"Men and women, Brother King." Sister Amelia gestured at her brethren. "The Shakers believe that the male and female principle are both present in our Maker. In other words, God is both man *and* woman, yet so much more, of course."

"If God is both, why do you split them up?"

"Because He did. Clearly it's a sign. We are not meant to live together. Nor, might I add, to sleep together."

Nate was compelled to point out a flaw in her reasoning. "If everybody did as you do, no babies would be born. The human race would die out in a few generations."

"And that's a bad thing?" Sister Amelia smiled. "Besides, we don't have that long left. Elder Lexington expects the Second Coming before the decade is out. There is no need for more babies."

Nate excused himself and walked to the male quarters. He knocked, but no one came. Figuring most of the men were busy elsewhere, he tried the latch. A musty, dark hall led past room after room. Each contained a bed and some a chair and a few a chest of drawers. At the far end a lamp glowed. Nate came up quietly and stopped in the doorway.

Arthur Lexington was on his knees, his eyes closed, his hands clasped to his chest. His lips moved in silent prayer.

Nate waited. At length Lexington lowered his hands and said aloud, "Amen." Nate coughed to get his attention.

"Brother King!" Lexington exclaimed, rising. "How long have you been standing there? What can I do for you?"

"I came to beat your head against the wall."

"I beg your pardon?"

Nate entered and straddled a chair. "I wasn't fooling about the Pawnees being out for blood."

"I never thought you were," Lexington responded.

"Then why haven't you taken my advice and posted lookouts? If you won't arm yourselves, at least do that much."

"Oh, Brother King," Lexington said in a tone that implied Nate was being silly. "Love thy neighbor, remember? Were we to post sentries it would betray our beliefs. We must trust in God and He will deliver us."

He went to a table and picked up his Bible. "In any event, by your own admission the Pawnees aren't after us. They are after *you*."

"That didn't stop them from killing the farmer I told you about, and that wrangler," Nate noted.

"I have faith, Brother King. I am firmly convinced that if we leave them alone, they will leave us alone."

A premonition came over Nate, a feeling that if he couldn't make Lexington understand, terrible things would happen. He tried to shrug it off as of no consequence, but he couldn't. "I could lend you my pistols. You could have two men keep watch down at the bend with orders to give the alarm if they so much as glimpse a painted face."

"You are persistent, Brother King. I will give you that. But we are talking in circles." Lexington moved to the window and parted the curtains, admitting sparkling shafts of sunlight. The window had no glass. "God is not to be trifled with. Either you believe or you don't. Either you abide by His will or you don't. We do. To us His will is everything. For me to post guards or to take arms is the same as saying we don't believe. We can't do that, Brother King. Not now. Not ever."

Nate stood. "I'll keep watch myself, then, until the freighters get here." He turned to go.

"Don't be mad."

"I don't want any of you dead because of me."

"It wouldn't be your fault. Each of us does what he has to. If it will make you feel better, I'll send someone with you. He won't use a gun and he won't resist if the savages attack, but he can keep you company."

"Forget it." Nate stalked out, simmering. He kept trying but it was like talking to a tree stump. Once outside, he stopped and stared at the gaping black maws of the cave and the bubbling springs and the steam rising into the air. His premonition worsened.

Something awful was going to happen.

It was only a matter of time.

Chapter Eleven

The religious ceremony was like nothing Nate ever saw. It was like nothing he ever imagined.

It started normally enough. The Shakers gathered between the log buildings, the women on one side, the men on the other, in rows. Arthur Lexington read from Scripture and expounded on what he read. The thrust of his message was that they must stand firm in their faith. They must remember that Adam tainted all mankind when he had relations with Eve.

"Sexual impurity is the root of all evil. Sexual impurity is the great sin. It was the reason for the Fall. But we have redeemed ourselves by refusing to succumb. We deny our carnal urges. We cast them aside and live as the Lord always meant for men and women to live, as equals, as brothers and sisters, with none of the taint of Adam's legacy.

"We must be strong. We must stay pure. We must resist temptation each and every moment. Always remember our eternal reward for staying true to our Lord's command to be perfect.

"Here, in our new home, we will build a reflection of that reward. We will have a heaven on earth, a place where we may live in peace, a place where the Lord reminds us of his love daily by the shaking of the ground under our feet."

Nate glanced at Jeremiah Blunt, who was seated cross-legged on his right. The freighters were gathered behind them. They had been permitted to watch but were not to interrupt or interfere in any way. Lexington was quite insistent, and Blunt had said he and his men would honor the request. "What does the shaking of the ground have to do with anything?" Nate quietly wondered.

"I have no idea," the captain confessed.

A few hymns were sung, each with increasing fervor. A lot of the Shakers swayed as they sang. Some raised their arms and cried out to their Maker. By the sixth song, all of them were swaying and stamping their feet. Then, as if with one mind, the Shakers began to move. They formed into concentric circles. In the center was a small circle of women, then a circle of men, then another circle of women, and last another circle of men. As they moved they raised their voices to the heavens and danced in short, rhythmic steps while waving their arms aloft. Many cried out as if in the grip of ecstasy.

Round and round the circles went, the inner clockwise, the next counterclockwise, the third again clockwise, the last as the second. They sang and they danced and they swayed. A spontaneous trembling broke out and spread from worshiper to worshiper so that soon all of them were shaking as they danced, quaking from head to toe, their faces aglow with spiritual rapture. The longer it went on, the more violent their shaking became. Halleluiahs and other cries pierced the air.

"I get it now," Jeremiah Blunt said.

So did Nate. The way they were quaking and trembling: exactly as the ground did. Arthur Lexington had taken it into his head that it was a sign. To Lexington and his followers, the Valley of Skulls was a special place where the earth under their feet moved as they did.

Nate gazed at a bubbling hot spring and at the steam rising from another, and was troubled.

On and on it went, the dancing and singing and shaking, ever more intense, ever more feverish. Suddenly a woman burst out shouting in a strange tongue. A man did the same but in a different tongue. Then others, all of them with their eyes closed and shaking violently, many of the women and a few of the men with tears trickling down their cheeks.

"It is a wonderment," Jeremiah Blunt declared.

Presently a woman collapsed, overcome by her ardor. Several others did likewise.

The fervor was at its peak.

Then, like a clock winding down, it began to slow. The songs became slower. The dancers slowed. The trembling and shaking slowed until finally the Shakers came to an exhausted stop. Drained yet beaming with joy, the women and the men again formed into their respective rows and turned sweat-stained faces to their leader, who had stepped out of the group to address them.

"Once again we have affirmed our love and our faith. Once again we have felt the Lord among us and in us. Now let each of us rest from our labors and partake of one another's company as equals and brethren."

The service came to an end. There was no hugging, no kissing, not even a shaking of hands. They looked on one another and smiled and spoke in soft voices.

Lexington came over to the freighters, Sister Amelia in his wake. "Well, gentlemen. What did you think of our service?"

"You are an amazing people," Jeremiah Blunt said.

"We do the Lord's will, nothing more," Lexington told him.

Sister Amelia stepped up. "If any of you have been moved to join us, we would gladly welcome you."

Several of the freighters laughed and Haskell said, "Ma'am, we thank you for the offer. But me, I'm a married man, and I couldn't live without that impurity you're not so fond of."

"Me, either," another man declared. "I buy it real regular when I'm in St. Louis."

More laughter caused Jeremiah Blunt to swivel and say, "That will be enough."

The freighters fell silent.

Arthur Lexington turned to Nate. "How about you, Brother King? Does our style of life appeal to you?"

"I'm married, too," Nate said.

"Marriage is no obstacle. Bring your wife, if you want. Of course, the two of you could never have relations again, but you're more than welcome."

"Marriage without sex?" a freighter blurted. "Where's the point in that?"

More laughter caused Blunt to say sternly, "When I say enough, I mean enough." He smiled at Lexington. "I'm afraid my men are too fond of their earthly ways to give them up."

"Suit yourselves, but we are always open to new members. Keep that in mind should any of you change yours."

The elder and his shadow went to mingle with the rest.

Blunt leaned toward Nate. "Are you as concerned by this as I am?"

"By the ceremony?"

"No. By this," Blunt said, and smacked the ground with his calloused hand. "By the damnable tremors."

As if that were a stage cue, the ground under them shook. Not hard, but enough that the horses in the corral pranced and whinnied and some of the oxen bellowed in fear.

"See?" Blunt said.

Lexington raised his arms aloft. "Did you feel that, Brother and Sisters? It was the Lord affirming our faith. Let us give thanks and praise that we have been led to this holy place."

"Holy, hell," a freighter scoffed.

Nate held his own counsel. According to the Indian legends, the ground in the valley had been shaking since any of the tribes could remember. The Shakers were welcome to call it the handiwork of the Lord if they wanted, but in his opinion shaking ground was, well, shaking ground.

"We'll spend tomorrow unloading," Jeremiah Blunt said. "I expect to leave by ten the next morning. Are you coming with us as far as Bent's Fort?"

Nate hadn't given it any thought, but he did dearly want to get home and be with his family. "I might go with you a short way and then strike off through the mountains."

The Shakers were dispersing. At Blunt's command, his men rose and walked toward the freight wagons, now parked near the Conestogas of their hosts.

Nate found himself alone, but he didn't stay that way. He sensed rather than heard someone come up behind him and went to turn.

"Don't look back," Maklin's voice came over his shoulder. "Wait until I head for the corral so they won't think I've spotted them and told you. Then come join me."

"They?" Nate said.

"The south side of the valley, the high cliff with five caves. Look at the very top, but don't let on that's what you're doing."

When the Texan didn't say more, Nate said, "Maklin?" but got no answer. Rising, he shifted enough to see him walking off. Nate stretched and pretended he had a cramp in his leg and raised it up and down a few times. As he did, he peered from under his eyebrows at the cliff Maklin mentioned. The cave mouths were awash in the red glow of the setting sun. The cliff itself was slate gray.

Nate saw nothing out of the ordinary. Not at first. He had to flick his gaze back and forth several times before he saw what Maklin had seen. He couldn't make out much detail at that distance but he didn't need to. He made for the corral.

Maklin was saddling his horse, his back to the cliff. "It will be dark before we get up there."

"The dark will work against them as much as it does us." Nate nodded toward a cluster of Shakers. "What puzzles me is you putting your life at risk for people you don't much care for."

"We have to do something or it will be my wife all over again, only worse. No one deserves that."

Nate was careful not to move with undue haste as he slid a bridle on the bay and then his blanket and saddle.

"I can ask Blunt for more men to go with us," Maklin suggested.

Shaking his head, Nate said, "The more who ride out, the more suspicious they'll be. Just the two of us, they might think we're going off to hunt." He led the bay from the corral, swung up, and poked his heels. No one called out to them. No one wondered where they were going.

"We'll have to do this smart," Maklin said as they neared the bend.

"I never do anything any other way if I can help it,"

Nate replied. Too often, though, what he took for smart turned out to be less so.

Once out of the Valley of Skulls, they rode straight on into the forest. As soon the canopy hid them, Nate reined to the south. He rode as fast as the terrain and the gathering twilight permitted.

The ground rose in a series of broad shelves to the canyon rim. Forest covered about half. The rest consisted of grassy belts broken here and there by boulder fields.

Nate avoided open ground as much as possible. The climb was steep and arduous, and often they stopped to scan the next stretch to be sure they didn't ride into an ambush.

"I'm surprised they came all this way," the Texan commented at one point when they were high up.

Nate wasn't. In the name of hate men drove themselves to deeds they wouldn't otherwise do.

"That one you called Kuruk must want you dead awful bad." Maklin echoed Nate's thought.

"The feeling is mutual." Nate wasn't a killer by nature. He only did it when he had to, when circumstances left him no choice. He had no choice now. He must slay Kuruk not only for his own sake but so that no one else lost their lives. The farmer and his family and the wrangler had died because of him; he would be damned if any more would.

The sun relinquished its reign to the mantle of darkness. Soon a crescent moon added its radiance to the shimmering of the stars.

Out of their dens and thicket hideaways came the fanged creatures of the night. Legions of predators were on the prowl in search of prey to fill their bellies. Their cries and howls and wails were constant, a bestial chorus that once heard was never forgotten.

The farther they climbed, the slower they went. Nate constantly tested the wind with his senses. It blew down off the heights in spurts. A gust would fan him and rustle the trees, and then everything would be still.

The rim was a black silhouette against the stars. They were several hundred feet below it when Nate drew rein and announced, "We'll go the rest of the way on foot."

Maklin didn't argue. Swinging lithely down, he tied his mount to a fir and loosened the pistols wedged under his belt. "We can cover more ground if we separate."

"We'd be easier to pick off, too." Nate preferred that they stick together so they could watch each other's back.

Maklin didn't argue.

Taking the lead, Nate rapidly climbed until he came to a stone wall fifteen to twenty feet high. He groped about him but couldn't find handholds. "This way," he whispered, and bore to the left, on the lookout for a gap or some other means of reaching the crest.

"Maybe they're not up here now," Maklin whispered. "It could be we came all this way for nothing."

Nate hoped not. He crept along until a puff of wind drew him to a split wide enough for a man to slide through. He had to turn sideways and wriggle. Intent as he was on not getting stuck, he forgot about his Hawken and bumped the stock against the rock. The sound was much too loud.

Nate came out on a flat rocky parapet. Crouching, he glided to the edge. Below lay the Valley of Skulls. Light showed in the windows and a fire had been kindled near the wagons.

"Any sign of them?" Maklin whispered.

Nate was about to say no when from off to their left,

as clear as could be, came a cough. Dropping into a crouch, he moved more warily than ever.

The cough was repeated.

Something about it troubled Nate. A boulder hove out of the pitch and he was making his way around it when he happened to glance up and saw a shape crouched on all fours. A long tail flicked and lashed.

The tail of a mountain lion.

Chapter Twelve

Nate King reacted in a twinkling. He whipped up his Hawken and started to thumb back the hammer. Even as he did, the cougar whirled with astounding speed and in a starlit tawny blur leaped off the other side of the boulder. It happened so fast that it took a few seconds for Nate to realize the cat had fled and not attacked him. "That was close," he breathed.

"What was?" Maklin whispered.

Nate twisted in the saddle. "You didn't see the mountain lion?"

"Where?"

"On that boulder."

"I was looking down there." Maklin's arm was a black bar, extended toward the Valley of Skulls. His voice dropped until Nate barely heard him. "Tell me I'm seeing things. Look over yonder and tell me what in God's name those are."

Puzzled, Nate turned. The valley floor was a mire of ink save for the lit windows and the fire by the corral. Across the valley reared the opposite heights. He looked, and his skin crawled with goose flesh. "I see them, too."

"What *are* they?"

Nate wished he knew. Pale *things* appeared to be moving down the mountain. Long and slender, they writhed like snakes. As he watched in stunned amazement, one of them changed shape, expanding until it was bloated at the middle and thin at both ends.

"Hell spawn," the Texan said.

A gust of wind fanned Nate's face. The next moment, the shapes did something even more wondrous; they broke apart. Each became two or three smaller shapes that continued to crawl and writhe.

"What *are* they?" Maklin said again.

Nate racked his brain for an explanation. That both he and the Texan saw them proved they weren't an illusion. That they moved as they did suggested they were alive. But if they were, they were creatures the likes of which mortal man had seldom set eyes on. Maybe—and his mind balked at the idea but it was the only one that made sense—maybe they were creatures from the Indian legends. Maybe they were the animals whose skulls and bones littered the valley floor.

Then, with disturbing abruptness, the pale shapes faded and were gone. One moment they were there, the next they weren't.

"What the hell?" Maklin blurted.

Nate searched in vain for further sign of them. When it became apparent they were gone, he shook his head and said, " 'There are more things in heaven and earth . . . ' "

"What was that?"

"A quote that a friend of mine likes to say a lot."

Maklin shifted toward him. "Damn. We forgot about the Pawnees."

Alarmed, Nate whipped around. The crest was still and quiet. As near as he could tell, they were the only two human beings atop the mountain. "They're gone."

"They were here, though. We both saw them."

Nate had seen *something* earlier. What he took to be the heads and shoulders of men spying on the valley's new inhabitants from on high. At that distance it had been impossible to say for certain that it was the Pawnees, but he was willing to bet his poke it was.

Nate dismounted and walked to where he could see the sweep of mountains to the south. At night the rolling tiers of forested slopes were a sea of ink, which was why the one bright orange finger stood out like a lighthouse beacon. "There."

"I reckon a mile, maybe less," Maklin guessed. "They must have been going down while we were coming up."

"Let's have a look-see."

They became tortoises. They had to be, for the sake of their animals as well as their own hides. The snap of a branch would carry on the wind. The peal of hooves, too, so they rode at a walk until the mile had become half a mile and then a quarter of a mile and finally they were a few hundred yards above the fire.

Nate drew rein. "I'll go. Wait here with the horses."

"Why just you?"

"One is quieter than two." Nate slid down and held the bay's reins for Maklin to take.

"It should be me. I don't have a wife and kids."

Nate whispered back, "You don't fool me anymore."

"What are you talking about?"

"Not now." Nate nodded toward the fire. "Whatever happens, stay with the horses. We can't afford to lose them."

"I don't like this."

"You don't have a wife and kids, true, but I know Pawnee," Nate explained. He didn't mention that he knew very little.

Pines reared in darkling ranks. The brush was thick and dry. Nate placed each moccasin as lightly as he could. Bent low, he stalked to within earshot.

They were there, all eleven Nate had previously

counted, hunkered around the small fire, talking in low tones. Kuruk was doing most of the talking. Only a few words reached Nate clearly and they were not enough to give him any idea of what the Pawnees were discussing.

Nate raised the Hawken. Kuruk was the key. Kuruk's hate had brought the rest. Were Kuruk to die they might decide to return to their village. Nate sighted down the barrel. He couldn't see the bead at the end, but he was sure he could hit Kuruk square in the chest and that should do the job.

Unexpectedly, a Pawnee rose and came toward the pines. He was scratching himself, down low. He came directly toward the spot where Nate was crouched and said something over his shoulder that caused some of the others to laugh.

Nate froze. He was far enough from the fire that he should be invisible. The warrior came closer and closer until he stopped barely ten feet away and hitched at his buckskins. Nate heard the splatter and smelled urine. He didn't so much as blink.

The warrior let out an "Ahhhhh." He said something to the others and they laughed again. Then he was done and turning and his face rose until he was staring right at Nate.

Nate held his breath. It would take exceptional eyesight to spot him.

The Pawnee paused. He bent forward and his hand rose to a knife on his hip. For fully half a minute he peered into the dark. At last he straightened and took his hand off the knife hilt and headed back to the fire.

Nate exhaled. That had been close. Quickly he took aim again only to find that the warrior was between him and Kuruk; he didn't have a clear shot. He raised his cheek from the stock, waiting for the warrior to sit back down. But the warrior didn't. Instead, he stopped and quietly said a few words, and the next moment they were all grabbing weapons and scrambling to their feet.

Nate whirled and ran.

Howling like wolves, the Pawnees were after him. Several had yanked burning brands from the fire and held them over their heads. The combined light was enough that one of them pointed and yelled to his companions.

Pumping his legs, Nate churned up the slope. The brush tore at him. Tree branches threatened to gouge his eyes. He had gone ten yards when he realized the mistake he was making and veered away from the horses and the Texan.

The Pawnees were in full throat, screeching and yipping and brandishing their bows and lances.

An arrow buzzed past Nate's ear. He dodged around a pine. Weaving, he ran harder. Another shaft thudded into a tree. He came to a flat stretch and poured on the speed only to be confronted by a dense thicket. Without hesitation he plunged in, lowering his head and throwing an arm in front of his face to protect his face and throat. He went eight or nine steps and stopped.

On both sides the thicket crackled and rustled to the passage of Pawnees. They had lost sight of him, but they knew he was in there somewhere. Kuruk barked commands.

Nate hunkered low. It was dark enough that a warrior could pass within a few feet and not spot him. So long as none of them ran smack into him, he might escape detection.

Then Kuruk switched to English. "I know you are in here, Grizzly Killer. I am not a fool. We will find you and we will kill you."

Nate peered through the thicket, hoping for a shot.

"How did you find us? We have been most careful in covering our tracks, as you whites would say."

Nate didn't take the bait. He stayed silent. Feet moved stealthily to his right. Legs appeared to his left. The warriors were so close he could practically reach out and touch them. They went on by.

Another warrior said something in Pawnee. Kuruk, forgetting himself, started to answer in English with, "He has to be. We would have heard him if—" Kuruk switched to Pawnee.

Nate raised his head. No one was near him. He was about to get out of there when the thicket parted and in front of him reared a warrior he hadn't noticed.

The Pawnee uttered a sharp cry and raised a lance.

Nate shot him. He hiked the Hawken and fired. The muzzle flash lit the warrior's painted face and betrayed his surprise at being shot through the heart. Heaving erect, Nate bolted. He burst out of the thicket and flew. A lance missed his shoulder. An arrow nicked the eagle feather in his hair.

After him came the Pawnees, yelling their war cries.

Kuruk bellowed something.

Nate considered himself to be fairly fleet of foot, but two of the Pawnees were as fast if not faster. A glance showed them hard after him and gaining. Neither let a shaft fly; evidently they intended to take him alive. Kuruk's doing, Nate suspected. Kuruk wanted to stake him out and torture him.

Nate tried to shake them. He cut back and forth at right angles. He weaved among benighted boles. The Pawnees not only kept up; they continued to gain. One of them called out to those behind.

Nate had lost his sense of direction. He wasn't sure which way he was running. He turned right.

From out of nowhere a warrior appeared. The man had a tomahawk and the instant he saw Nate, he raised it to cleave Nate's skull. In the span of a heartbeat Nate had a flintlock out. He fired and sidestepped as the tomahawk descended. Another second and he was in the clear while the warrior flopped and gurgled. He jammed the spent pistol under his belt and sprinted full out.

Kuruk was shouting again, sounding beside himself.

Nate ran. He was growing winded, but he could last a good while yet. He nearly tripped over a log. A boulder almost broke both legs. He took two more bounds and suddenly he was falling. He had gone over a bank. It was a short drop, but he hit hard enough to knock the wind out of him. Tumbling, he wound up in high grass. He lay there catching his breath while around him the night was broken by yells and the beat of moccasin-clad feet.

They had lost him again. They were searching, roving from side to side. A figure appeared on top of the bank. It was Kuruk, overseeing the hunt.

Nate felt at his waist for the other flintlock. He wrapped his fingers around the wood and went to tug it free.

Almost at his elbow another figure materialized. The Pawnee was staring ahead, not at the ground, and went by in a rush.

Nate looked at the bank. Kuruk was gone. Nate stayed where he was while the sounds of pursuit faded. The Pawnees had gone on down the mountain. For the moment he was safe. Or was he? Nate wouldn't put it past the wily Kuruk to be lurking close by in the hope Nate would give himself away. Silently, Nate made it to his knees. Silently and slowly, he stood.

No outcries split the night.

Nate sought the North Star. It would tell him where he was. By his reckoning, the Texan and the horses were to the northeast. After all the running he had done, the climb taxed him. He skirted the Pawnee camp and would have kept on climbing had one of the Pawnee horses not nickered. A brainstorm struck, and he quickly wheeled. Every animal had been hobbled so it couldn't stray off. Drawing his bowie knife, Nate cut the first hobble and then the second. Once they were all free he would spook them and leave the Pawnees stranded afoot.

Nate moved to the third horse. He bent, and saved his life. A lance speared the space where his chest had been. He spun as a warrior sprang. A knife sought his neck. He grabbed the Pawnee's wrist and the Pawnee gripped his. Locked together, they struggled furiously, each seeking to wrest loose and stab the other. The Pawnee was shorter, but he was broad at the shoulders and immensely strong. For long seconds the outcome hung in the balance. Then the unforeseen occurred; Nate blundered into the fire. He felt intense heat. Searing pain shot up his legs. Instinctively he tried to leap back, but the Pawnee held him fast and grinned a vicious grin. The pain worsened. Smoke was rising from Nate's moccasins and his pants. He was about to burst into flame.

Exerting all his strength, Nate wrenched and flung the Pawnee from him. The warrior was up in a heartbeat. His knife held low, the man came in low and quick, slashing at Nate's groin. A twist and a step and Nate sank the bowie to the hilt between two ribs.

The Pawnee's back arched and his mouth gaped wide, but no sounds came out. He gulped breath, or tried to, and died.

Nate yanked the bowie out as the warrior fell. A

shout warned him others were converging. Spinning, he got out of there. His feet hurt from the flames and each stride made him grimace. But he didn't slow. He ran until he was near where he thought Maklin should be, but the horses and the Texan weren't there. For a panicked instant Nate thought Maklin had run out on him. He should have known better.

Hooves drummed and a strong hand gripped Nate by the arm and swung him onto the bay. Side by side they rode for their lives while behind them the Pawnees rent the air with yowls of frustration.

"Thanks," Nate said.

"We're not safe yet."

A glance at their camp showed Nate several had mounted and were giving chase.

Chapter Thirteen

Nate reined down the mountain. The Texan's pistol boomed and the Pawnees howled in rage.

The ride was a nightmare. Obstacles loomed so abruptly that avoiding them took all the skill Nate possessed. His fear was for the bay more than himself. A mistake on his part could bring the animal to ruinous harm.

They rode and they rode and gradually the sounds of pursuit faded. They were nearly to the bottom of the mountain when Nate brought the bay to a stop and shifted in the saddle to listen.

"I think we shook them," Maklin said.

"I hope so."

"How many did you rub out?"

Nate had to think. "I shot two and stabbed another. I expect all three are dead."

"And I shot a fourth, so there are only seven left. Maybe Kuruk will give up and go home."

"Anyone who hates as much as he does won't quit easy." Nate clucked the weary bay on.

Maklin came up next to him. "What do you think those things were we saw earlier?"

"I have no idea," Nate admitted. But he was determined to find out. "I reckon a visit to those caves is in order."

"When you do, I'm tagging along."

Nothing else was said until they neared the Valley

of Skulls. The weary bay was about tuckered out and Nate was looking forward to letting it rest.

Suddenly a voice split the night.

"Halt! Who is that?"

Nate drew rein in surprise. "Haskell, is that you? It's King and Maklin. We're coming in."

The freighter lieutenant and another man had their rifles in hand. "It's good to see you safe. We heard shooting far off, so the captain decided to have us take turns standing guard until morning."

Nate related, briefly, the clash with the Pawnees.

"We'll keep our eyes skinned. If those devils show their red hides, we'll blister them with lead."

The valley lay still and peaceful under the stars. Most of the freighters had turned in, but Jeremiah Blunt was still up and Nate had to recite his fight again between sips of piping-hot coffee.

"We'll inform Lexington in the morning," Blunt declared. "His people are at risk."

"Not that it will do any good," Maklin said bitterly. "Not one of those yacks will lift a finger to defend themselves."

"The Pawnees don't know that," Blunt mentioned.

Nate hadn't thought of that. Since most whites carried guns, Kuruk would assume the Shakers were armed and might not attack. "It could be what saves them," he said, and was raising his tin cup for another swallow when he went rigid.

The ground was shaking. Not hard, not violently, but enough that Nate felt uneasy. The horses set to whinnying and the oxen to lowing. A nearby cauldron bubbled loudly and a prolonged hiss filled the air. In less than a minute the shaking stopped.

"I don't like it when it does that," Jeremiah Blunt

said. "I am not a student of geology, but I know when ground is unstable. The Shakers would be well advised to set up their new colony elsewhere."

Nate agreed, but he mentioned that trying to convince Arthur Lexington would be a waste of breath.

"The man is too fond of himself. He believes he is right and everyone else is wrong."

"People like him rub me wrong," Maklin said.

At last Nate was able to turn in. He lay on his back with his saddle for a pillow. Every muscle seemed sore. He was so tired he figured he would drift off quickly, but his mind refused to shut down. It was three in the morning when sleep claimed him.

The clink of a coffeepot woke him. Dawn was about to break and Blunt and several others were already up. Blunt planned to start unloading the wagons as soon as the sun rose in order to get it done in one day.

Nate offered to lend a hand, but the captain said it wasn't necessary, that his men had strong backs and worked well together.

Along about ten, with the freighters unloading and the Shaker men busy building and the Shaker women doing their daily chores, Nate decided to explore the rest of the valley. He drifted past the cabins, then past hot springs too numerous to count. Some constantly bubbled and boiled while others bubbled now and again. When they did, they hissed like serpents.

Nate noticed a foul odor that was stronger near the cauldrons and vents.

The skulls and bones fascinated him. There were so many. Their size staggered the imagination. One leg bone was bigger than he was. A skull had teeth longer than his fingers. Whatever these creatures were, they had been huge.

Slopes sparse with vegetation led up to the cliffs. Nate counted over forty on the north side of the valley alone. An ancient footpath wound up to them.

Nate stood in the entrance to the lowest and peered into its depths. The reek was strong here, too, although why that should be puzzled him. He started in, but had only gone a dozen steps when it became so dark he couldn't see his hand at arm's length. He deemed it best to back out and was about to do so when he heard the unmistakable tread of a foot.

Someone, or some thing, was in there with him.

Nate raised the Hawken. The Indians claimed that the race that once lived in the valley had long since died out, but maybe the Indians were mistaken.

"King? Are you in here?"

Lowering his rifle, Nate answered, "I'm coming out, Maklin." He felt like a fool. Even more so when he nearly bumped into the Texan. "What are you doing here?"

"I told you I wanted to tag along. Blunt saw you hike off and let me know."

"He would make a fine wife."

The Texan grinned. "Don't let him hear you say that. I've seen him lift an anvil over his head." He stared into the dark tunnel. "So what did you find in there? Anything?"

"No."

The trail continued upward, a groove in the rock worn by untold thousands of feet untold thousands of years ago.

"Any sign of those things we saw last night?"

"Not yet."

The next cave was smaller. The cave floor was inches thick with dust and the cave had a musty smell. The sun penetrated into it far enough to reveal bones scattered all over. Only they were different from those below.

"These were people," Maklin said.

The dome of a skull poked from the dust. Nate picked it up and brushed it off and turned it over. It was twice the size of an ordinary skull and the eye sockets were twice the size of human eyes. Patches of red hair clung to the crown. He plucked at a strand and it broke apart. The jaw was intact, and when he examined the mouth, he received a shock. "Maybe not."

"What have you got there?"

Nate showed Maklin the skull and touched a finger to the mouth. "You tell me."

"I'll be damned."

The mouth was rimmed with two rows of teeth on both the top and bottom. All were the same size and shape, unlike a human mouth where the back teeth were different from the front. Each tooth was as big as Nate's thumbnail, the enamel still strong after all the years the skull must have lain there.

"It has to be a freak of some kind," Maklin guessed.

Nate roved about and found a smaller skull. A child's, if the size was an indication. It, too, had two rows of teeth, top and bottom. He showed it to the Texan.

"These people were monsters."

Tufts of red hair poked from the child's skull, too. Nate touched one and said, "Some Indian tribes have tales of a time long ago when redheaded cannibals lived in the mountains. They say they fought with the cannibals and eventually wiped them out."

Maklin picked up the large skull. "These were those cannibals, you reckon?" He held it in one hand. "I heard a lot of strange tales myself from the Lipans and others." He drew one of his knives.

"What are you doing?"

"No one will believe me if I don't have something to show them." So saying, Maklin pried a tooth loose and slid it into a pocket. "The Lipans wouldn't like that. They're afraid to disturb the dead. They think the spirits of the dead can come back from the land of the dead to haunt us." The Texan chuckled. "I loved Na-lin dearly, but her superstitions were plumb ridiculous."

They emerged into the light of day. Nate craned his neck to scan the caves higher up. Nowhere was there sign of life, nowhere a clue to the pale things he had seen the night before.

"Are you fixing to climb all the way to the top?"

Nate was thinking about it. He would like to know if there were more skulls with two rows of teeth. He started up but stopped at an exclamation from Maklin.

"Will you look at that!"

The Texan was staring at the mountain rim to the south. There, clearly outlined against the blue of sky, stood a lone figure. Nate didn't have his spyglass, but it had to be one man and one man only. "Kuruk."

"The bastard is letting you know he's still out there."

Nate turned and made for the bottom. A gauntlet had been thrown in his face, and he accepted.

"Hold on, hoss. What's the rush?"

"I aim to end it," Nate vowed. "One way or the other."

"Think a moment. That's exactly what he wants you to do. Go hurrying off to find him and ride right into a trap."

"Could be," Nate allowed.

"You're going anyway?"

"If I don't I'll be looking over my shoulder the rest of my days." Nate refused to let that happen.

"I savvy. You're worried he might follow you to that

valley where you live and do harm to your missus and your kids and friends."

"Something like that."

"Well, then. We'll go to where they camped last night and track them down. It will be them or us."

"Not us. Me."

"I have my orders, remember."

Nate went in search of Jeremiah Blunt. The captain was busy overseeing the transfer of crates and goods from the wagons to the cabins. Tools, salt, flour, blankets, the Shakers had enough of everything to last years. Nate tapped Blunt on the shoulder. "We need to talk."

"I'm listening," Blunt said, and in the next breath bellowed, "Williams! Careful with that. It has china plates and dishes. Drop it and you'll wish you hadn't."

"The Texan," Nate said.

"What about him?" Blunt asked, and turned to a man carrying a pack. "That one goes in the women's quarters. You're not to go in yourself. Just hand it to them at the door."

"Call off your shadow. I have something to do and I'm doing it alone."

"Can't," Blunt said.

"Why in hell not?"

"Now, now. Don't lose your temper. I can't and I won't because I like your daughter."

"What does Evelyn have to do with this?"

Blunt faced him. "The night before she left with McNair, she asked me to watch out for you."

"She did what?"

Blunt grinned. "She's your daughter. She loves you. All that talk about the Valley of Skulls worried her so much, she took me aside and asked if I would do what I could to make sure you get back to your family safe and sound."

Nate sighed. It sounded like something Evelyn would do. Behind his back, no less. In that, she was much like her mother. Winona, too, had a mind of her own and was not shy about having her say and doing as she pleased.

"A promise is a promise," Jeremiah Blunt said. "Where you go, Maklin goes. What you do, he does. That's how it will be until we part company."

"Why him out of all your men? Just because he's killed?"

"I figured you had a lot in common. You've lived with Indians. He's lived with Indians. You like the wilds. He likes the wilds. And when I asked for a volunteer he raised his hand."

"Why?"

"You'd have to ask him."

Nate cradled his Hawken. "I'm putting my foot down. He's not to come with me. I mean it."

"You can't stop him short of shooting him, and you won't do that. It's not in you." Blunt clapped Nate on the arm. "Cheer up. You're a good man, Nate King. A decent man. You put your family before all else. You treat others with respect so long as they respect you. You don't drink much and you hardly ever swear. Truth is, you're different from about every other mountain man I've met."

"There must be a lot of men like me."

Blunt sobered and shook his head. "I wish there were. A lot of men find goodness boring. They'd rather drink whenever they want and bed any woman they want and they don't give much of a damn about anyone but themselves."

Nate had more to say, but just then hooves clomped and up rode Maklin leading the bay by the reins.

"I'm ready to shed blood when you are, pard."

Chapter Fourteen

The Pawnee camp was deserted, the charred embers of their fire long gone cold.

Nate expected as much. Still, he took precautions. He drew rein a quarter of a mile below and climbed the rest of the way on foot, Maklin at his side every step.

"Where do you reckon they got to?"

Nate cast about for sign. Their horses had left plenty. The tracks pointed to the southwest.

"That's damn peculiar. I thought Pawnee country is to the east."

"It is."

"Then why the blazes are they heading southwest?" the Texan wondered.

Nate wondered, too. Given Kuruk's wily nature, there was no predicting what he was up to.

They retraced their steps to their mounts and began the hunt in earnest. And what a difference the sun made. Nate could hold to a rapid gait with little threat from logs and boulders and low limbs.

The Pawnees had ridden hard, which mystified him. They weren't running away. Kuruk wouldn't give up so long as breath remained in his body, and the other warriors would want revenge for their fallen friends. It was almost as if they were in a hurry to get somewhere.

Nate had assumed they didn't know the country, but maybe he was wrong. Maybe they had been there before.

Another possibility occurred to him. Maybe after last night Kuruk expected Nate and a lot of other whites to come after them. Maybe the Pawnees were riding hard to find a spot to spring an ambush.

The tracks entered a dense forest of mainly spruce. A thick carpet of fallen needles muffled their hoof falls. No other sounds pierced the quiet. Not the warble of a bird or the chatter of a squirrel.

A disturbing sign. Nate held the Hawken across his saddle. Here was as good a place as any for the Pawnees to strike. Maklin evidently felt the same; he rode with a hand on one of his silver-inlaid pistols.

Nothing happened. They emerged from the shadowed woodland into a sunny meadow. Several blacktailed does fled. Two cow elk stared and then imitated the does.

The tracks led across the meadow into tall firs. Here, the shadows were deeper. Once again the wild creatures were unusually quiet.

The short hairs at the nape of Nate's neck prickled. He would almost swear unseen eyes were watching. They went another mile and came on a clear ribbon of water. The tracks showed that the Pawnees had stopped to let their horses drink. Nate did the same. He scoured the brush, ready to seek cover at the first hint of danger. But all he saw moving was a butterfly.

"I don't like this, hoss," Maklin commented.

"Makes two of us."

"I have the feeling we're being led around by the nose like a bull on a rope."

"Makes two of us," Nate said again.

The Pawnees had stuck to the stream bank even though the waterway twisted and turned like a crazed snake. It made for slow going, another puzzlement given that until now the Pawnees had been riding like Mohawk-topped bats out of Hades.

Nate began to have second thoughts. There was just him and the Texan against seven warriors. Many a man had fallen prey to his own overconfidence, and he could be another.

The firs were so close together that at times there was barely space for the bay to pass between them. It gave Nate a feeling of being hemmed in. He never knew but when a Pawnee might pop out from behind one of the trees and let fly with a barbed shaft.

Another mile, and still nothing happened.

Maklin cleared his throat to ask a question. "Do you reckon this Kuruk wants to take you alive?"

"He's said as much," Nate said. "The better to torture me. Why?"

"Less chance of you taking an arrow between the shoulder blades."

The tracks climbed. In due course they were out of the firs and at the edge of a broad tableland dotted with stands of pine and deciduous trees interspersed with grassland. A park, the old-timers would call it. As picturesque as a painting.

"This makes no damn sense," Maklin grumbled.

Nate relaxed a bit. There was nowhere for the Pawnees to hide except the stands, and the track didn't go anywhere near them. In one a robin was singing. He spied movement in the high grass, but it was only a gray fox running for cover.

A mile more brought them to an unusual sight that high up in the mountains: a buffalo wallow. At one time buffalo had been common in the mountains. Shaggier cousins of their prairie brethren, they hid in deep thickets during the day, coming out at dawn and dust to graze. The wallow was old and had not seen use in a long time.

Nate skirted it as the Pawnees had done. He went perhaps fifty yards and came on another. Soon he passed a third and then a fourth. Once a sizeable herd had called the tableland home.

Maklin had been content to stay behind Nate, but now he brought his horse alongside the bay. "How much farther before we turn back?"

"I never said we were."

The Texan frowned. "I wish you had told me."

"It makes a difference?"

"I didn't count on staying out all night. Blunt is leaving tomorrow, and if I'm not there he might head out without me."

"You can turn back if you want and no hard feelings," Nate assured him. He didn't add that he hadn't wanted the help anyway.

"I don't run out on a pard. I can always catch up to the freight wagons. Those oxen are molasses with hide on."

A glint of light in the distance caused Nate to draw rein. He took out the spyglass. At the tableland's western boundary rose a serrated ridge heavy with growth. Beyond, slopes rose like stepping-stones to the Divide. Fully half a dozen peaks glistened white with snow.

"Anything?" Maklin asked.

"It's peaceful," Nate responded.

"Too much so. I feel like a cat in a roomful of rocking chairs."

Nate shortened the telescope and put it back in his parfleche and rode on. He thought of Winona and how much he missed her. Another wallow appeared on the right, its bottom mired in shadow.

"Notice anything about the tracks?" Maklin asked, interrupting Nate's reverie.

Nate glanced down. The prints were still in single file, their depth corresponding to the softness of the soil. "They're not riding fast anymore."

"Not that. They're going from wallow to wallow as if they're looking for something."

The notion struck Nate as humorous. The only thing in wallows was dirt. The buffalo liked to urinate in it and then roll around to cake their hides and ward off flies and other pests.

Belatedly, the notion dawned on Nate that maybe the Pawnees weren't looking for something *in* the wallows. Maybe they were looking for a wallow deep enough to hide in. Even as the thought crossed his mind, a shadow at the bottom exploded into motion and hurtled up over the edge at him.

Nate's Hawken was pointing the other way. He had no time to turn it to shoot, but he did raise it to ward off a flash of steel. The warrior drew back the knife to stab again. There was a *crack* behind them and a hole appeared in the Pawnee's temple while simultaneously the other side of his head burst in a shower of skin and bone and blood.

The warrior staggered a few steps and fell.

Nate jerked the Hawken up, but there was no one else to shoot. The man had been the only one in the wallow. The high grass was undisturbed. He glanced back at Maklin and the smoking pistol in Maklin's hand. "Thanks."

"I was a shade slow."

Only after Nate was sure no others were going to attack did he climb down and roll the dead warrior over.

"Why just this one? Why not all of them at once?"

"Your guess is as good as mine would be." So much for Nate's idea that Kuruk would try to take him alive. He scanned the tableland ahead. "Could be they thought there would be more of us and they didn't want to risk all of them getting killed."

"So it'll be one at a time from here on out? Hell."

"We'll just have to keep on our toes."

"We can always turn back," Maklin said. "Make them come for you instead of us riding into every ambush they set."

"No."

"You're a stubborn cuss, Nate King."

Nate looked at him. "I want to end it."

"I don't blame you. But it will eat at your nerves, something like this." Maklin regarded the dead man, and grinned. "Look at the bright side. One more down means only six to go. The odds get better all the time."

They pressed on. White puffs of clouds floated serenely in the blue arc of sky. A breeze rippled the grass as it might waves in the sea. A pair of finches flew overhead and a doe and her fawn stared but didn't run off.

This was always the way with the wilderness. On the surface it could be as calm as a lake on a windless day. Under the surface, though, lurked perils galore. Beasts that delighted in feasting on human flesh. Snakes with poison in their fangs, scorpions with poison in their tails. Pitfalls of chance and deadfalls of trees and just plain falls for the unwary. So many dangers the list was too long for Nate to ponder.

The dark underbelly belied the warmth of the sun and the caress of the wind. A man must never forget the duality of the wilds or the wilds would lay that man low.

It was said that Nature was fickle. It was said that "she" was a harsh mistress. Nature had no gender, though. Nature was the order of things, and that order was a doe and her fawn on one hand and a Pawnee with a knife on the other. Life and death, light and dark, peaceful and violent.

Nate had thought about it and thought about it and concluded that if the order of things was a reflection of the Maker of that order, then the Maker must have a reason for things being as they were. But what that reason could be was as much a mystery now as it had been years ago when he first thought about it.

The best explanation he'd heard was courtesy of Shakespeare. Life was a forge, McNair once said, and just as the heat of a forge tempered metal to be hard so it wouldn't break, so, too, did life temper men and women to make them strong and wise so they wouldn't break under the adversities.

Nate gave a toss of his head. He was letting his mind wander again. That could prove costly should another Pawnee spring out of nowhere.

The sun was on its westward descent. Gradually the shadows lengthened. Nate began to cast about for a suitable camp and chose a stand of aspens. The trees would shelter them from the wind and hide their fire from the Pawnees. He climbed down and led the bay to a small clear space.

Maklin offered to gather firewood and walked off.

While he waited Nate gathered dry leaves and grass for kindling. He formed a pile, and when Maklin returned, took his fire steel and flint from his possibles bag. It took three strikes. Once the spark ignited, he puffed lightly on the tiny flame. As it grew he added fuel, and soon they had a crackling fire.

Maklin chewed on jerky and stared across at him.

"Something on your mind?"

"You wouldn't listen if there is."

"Try me."

"This is a mistake. I keep saying it, but you won't heed."

"Not that again."

Maklin bit off another piece. "You told me a while back that you had me figured out. Well, I have you figured out, too. You take the blame for Wendell and his family. You take the blame for our wrangler. You want revenge for them as much as Kuruk wants revenge for his uncle."

"If that's how you see it."

"You must not care for your family as much as you claim you do."

Nate's head snapped up. "Be careful. They are everything to me. I won't have anyone say otherwise."

"Your idea of everything must be different from mine or you wouldn't be doing this. You wouldn't make it this easy for your enemies to make your woman a widow and your boy and girl fatherless."

"That's going too far."

"I'm only saying my piece. If it hurts, then it's true, and if it's true you can't hold it against me."

Nate spent the next half hour examining his feelings. He decided the Texan was only half right, but even half was too much. He *did* feel bad about the Wendells and the wrangler. He *did* feel partly at fault. And, God help him, he *did* want Kuruk to be held to account. He gazed over the fire. "About what you said a while ago. I'm trying to do what's right."

"What's right isn't always what's best."

In his mind's eye Nate pictured Winona and Evelyn and Zach. "You have convinced me."

"I have?"

"We'll head back in the morning."

"You give your word?"

"If Kuruk wants me, he'll have to come after me."

"You're not as hardheaded as I thought."

"Maklin?"

"Yes?"

"Thanks."

Nate smiled and the Texan smiled and their bond of friendship was cemented. But the moment didn't last.

From out of the dark flew a swarthy warrior. With a fierce yip he swung the tomahawk at the Texan's head and then he vaulted the flames and threw himself at Nate.

Chapter Fifteen

Nate King hurled his coffee in the Pawnee's face. It didn't stop him, but it slowed him for the fraction of an instant Nate needed to dive to one side. The tomahawk cleaved air and the warrior whirled and came at him again.

Scrambling back, Nate dodged a blow to the neck and another to the face. He pushed to his feet, freeing his own tomahawk as he rose. Ducking under a slash that would have taken his head off, he swiped his tomahawk up and in, intending to open the Pawnee from navel to sternum. But the man was incredibly quick and sprang out of reach.

They paused, their eyes locked, taking each other's measure.

Uttering a war whoop, the warrior attacked again. Nate parried several swift swings and retaliated, but his blow was blocked. They circled, unleashing blow and counterblow. The sharp edge of the Pawnee's weapon missed Nate's neck by a whisper. Nate's next swing opened the Pawnee's arm.

Again they paused. The warrior crouched and moved his tomahawk in small circles, a mocking grin on his face. Nate waited, balanced on the balls of his feet. He had noticed that when the Pawnee came at him the last two times, the man's first blow was from right to left. Nate could use that against him.

Once more the warrior attacked. Once more his tomahawk arced from right to left.

Nate was ready. He swept his up and under and nearly severed the warrior's wrist. Shocked, the warrior swooped his other hand to a knife at his hip, but he didn't quite have it out of its sheath when Nate did to the man's neck as he had just done to the wrist.

Avoiding the spurting blood, Nate dashed to Maklin. The Texan was on his belly, his hat off, scarlet matting his hair. Nate sank to a knee and carefully rolled him over, fearing he would find Maklin's skull had been cleaved like a melon. He smiled in relief. Evidently the flat of the Pawnee's tomahawk had struck a glancing blow. There was a gash but nothing worse.

The Texan groaned and his eyes opened. "What the hell?"

"It was a Pawnee. He's dead."

Maklin winced and looked around and saw the dead warrior. "Good riddance. He damn near did me in."

"He was in a rush to get at me." Nate helped the Texan to sit up. "I have some herbs. I'll bandage you."

Gingerly touching the gash, Maklin swore. "All I need is some water to wash it clean." He glared at the one responsible. "I told you it would be one at a time."

"At least there are only five left."

"All it takes is one with luck." Maklin drew a handkerchief from a pocket and pressed it to his head. "Kuruk must figure to wear you down. What do you want to bet he'll be the last to try you?"

Nate dragged the body out of the firelight and rolled it into a patch of brush. That would have to do. He wasn't about to go to the time and effort to bury a man who had just tried to kill him.

Maklin was dabbing his wound. "I've been thinking. Why not treat them to their own medicine?"

"I'm listening."

"When we head back they're bound to follow. We

find a spot to wait for them and ambush the bastards like they've been ambushing us. Between the two of us we can end it, permanent."

"It's me they're after," Nate reminded him. "You don't need to get involved."

"Like hell I don't." Maklin held out his handkerchief, bright red with his blood. "They are out to get me now as much as they are out to get you. So what do you say? Tit for tat?"

The idea appealed to Nate. If they set this up right, the Pawnees would ride into their gun sights and it would be over.

"Then it's agreed? Good. I'm sick and tired of this cat and mouse. It will be root hog or die."

Once more Nate slept fitfully. It didn't help that the night was filled with the howls and roars of the meat-eaters out to fill their bellies and the screams and shrieks of the host of creatures that didn't want to fill them. Ordinarily they wouldn't disturb his slumber. But his frayed nerves were strained by every sound, no matter how slight, and he would wake with a start at each yowl and bleat.

The night seemed to last forever. A pink tinge had yet to color the eastern horizon when Nate decided enough was enough and cast off his blankets. Rekindling the fire, he put coffee on to brew. He needed it to help him stay awake. Dozing in the saddle could prove fatal.

The Texan didn't stir until a golden crown lent a regal touch to the new day. Sitting up, he yawned and stretched and said matter-of-factly, "You look like hell, hoss."

"I could use a good night's sleep," Nate admitted.

"It won't be long," Maklin predicted. "Maybe today we'll get to surprise your friend Kuruk."

Nate hoped so. After six cups of coffee and pemmican he was ready to head out. The day was bright and gorgeous as only days in the mountains could be. They retraced their steps across the tableland and came to the wallow where the warrior had attacked Nate.

"The body is gone." Maklin stated the obvious. "His friend must have carried him off."

"Something did," Nate said, and pointed at bits of buckskin and pieces of skin and hair that led off into the high grass.

"A bear, you reckon?"

Nate spied fresh tracks in the dirt. "Wolves. They found it during the night."

"I didn't think wolves ate people."

"Usually no. But if they're hungry enough or so old they can't get much to eat and they sniff out fresh blood . . ." Nate shrugged.

By noon they were in heavy forest. Shadows cloaked the undergrowth. Nate nearly put a crick in his neck from twisting and turning his head so much. He was glad that the next slope had a lot fewer trees. It had boulders, all shapes and sizes, scattered as if tossed by a giant hand.

Maklin was in the lead, his hat pushed back on his head so it didn't irritate his wound. "I sure do miss Texas. You ever been there?"

"No."

"You should visit it someday. Most who come never want to leave. It beats Lexington's Second Eden all hollow."

Nate couldn't shake the feeling they were being stalked. He turned to check behind them and saw his shadow and the bay's and the shadow of a giant boulder they were near—and another shadow seemingly took wing above them. Only it was much larger than any bird and it didn't have wings.

Nate swung around. He tried to raise the Hawken, but only had it halfway up when a stocky Pawnee slammed into him. The warrior had been on *top* of the boulder.

The impact tore Nate from the saddle. Steel nicked his shoulder as he slammed onto his back hard enough to jar his marrow. The knife rose and came down again, but he jerked aside and it bit into the dirt instead of his body. Driving his knee up, Nate dislodged his attacker. He still had the Hawken and when the warrior hissed and came at him in a frenzy of bloodlust, he swung with all the power in his shoulders and arms.

At the *thunk* of wood on bone, the Pawnee collapsed like a limp washcloth.

Maklin had reined around and drawn a pistol. "Is he dead?"

"I hope not." Quickly, Nate got his rope and cut off a short piece to bind the warrior's ankles. He didn't bind the hands. He stripped the Pawnee of weapons, squatted, and smacked the man's cheek several times. Ever so slowly, consciousness returned. The warrior looked about in confusion, saw Maklin with a pistol trained on him, and scowled.

Nate's fingers flowed in sign language. "Question. You called?"

The warrior didn't reply. He appeared to be in his late twenties or early thirties and had streaks of black and red war paint on his face.

Nate tried again. "Question. You called?" This time he added, "I no kill you talk."

The warrior glanced at Maklin, then at Nate. His hands rose. "I called Elk Horn."

"I called Grizzly Killer."

"I know. I wait kill you."

"Where Kuruk." Nate actually used the signs for "man called Bear."

The Pawnee's hands stayed on his chest.

"I want end fight," Nate signed. "I want fight Kuruk man and man." Among some tribes a personal challenge had to be accepted or the man who was challenged bore the taint of cowardice.

"Question. Why."

"I may-be-so kill him. Him may-be-so kill me. You and warriors go Pawnee land." Nate was offering to end it one way or the other. He held little hope they would accept and the warrior's attitude dashed it. The man's face hardened and his next movements were sharp and angry.

"You kill Beaver Tail. You kill Horse Running. You kill Shoots Two Arrows. Now we kill you."

"Question. No peace among us."

"You enemy," Elk Horn signed savagely. "No peace now, no peace tomorrow."

It was the same as saying that as far as the Pawnees were concerned, they wouldn't stop trying to rub Nate out while they were still on this side of the grave. Nate sighed and signed, "I try be friend."

Maklin had been watching intently. "That's why you let him live? I could have told you it wouldn't work."

"I'm not fond of killing."

"Sometimes a man has to. He isn't given a choice. Remember that talk we had about seeing your family again? You better accept you are in this to kill or you won't."

The hatred in the Pawnee's eyes was eloquent proof the Texan was right.

Nate drew his bowie and cut the rope around the

warrior's ankles. Then he slid the knife into its sheath and signed. "You go now."

"What are you doing?" Maklin demanded.

"I won't shoot an unarmed man." Nate stood, snagging the Hawken as he rose.

"Damn it, pard. He'll only try to kill you again."

"We're letting him go," Nate insisted.

The warrior was looking from one of them to the other. He coiled his legs and sat up.

"Blunt is right about you. You're too damn decent for your own good. But I can't let you do this."

Nate stepped between them. "I said he could go and I'm a man of my word. Lower your flintlock."

Maklin just sat there.

"I'm asking you as a friend."

With great reluctance, the Texan let the pistol sink to his side.

"Thank you." Nate glanced over his shoulder and saw that the warrior was rising. He smiled to show the man had nothing to fear, but the man didn't return it. Hate was writ on every particle of his face. "Go," Nate said, and motioned.

The Pawnee started to turn. Suddenly he lunged and scooped up his knife. With a cry of elation he leaped at Nate, the blade poised for a death stroke.

Maklin's pistol cracked.

The ball missed Nate's shoulder by an inch and cored the warrior's eye. The *splat* was followed by the thud of the body hitting the ground.

"So much for being nice."

Nate stared at the body. He was sick of this, sick of the death. "I forgot about his knife lying there."

"I didn't."

"You expected him to try again, didn't you?"

"Let's just say it didn't surprise me."

Nate looked up. "I'm in your debt again."

Maklin chuckled. "One of us had to use his head. And then there were four."

Nate went to climb on the bay. "His horse must be nearby. We should look for it."

They did, with no success. They did find tracks, though.

"Look here," Maklin said. "The rest rode off and took his animal with them." He scratched his chin. "I wonder how they got in front of us. I'd have sworn they must be miles to the southwest by now."

"They saw us turn back and circled around," Nate speculated. "It must have taken some hard riding."

"I've said it before and I'll say it again. They sure do want you dead."

On that grim note they rode on. By late afternoon they were within a mile of the Valley of Skulls. Both they and their horses were worn out.

Nate was surprised the Pawnees hadn't tried again, and mentioned as much.

"They've lost too many warriors," Maklin said. "They'll be more choosy about how they do it from here on out."

Suddenly their horses whinnied and shied. Nate heard a rumbling and realized the ground under them was shaking. It lasted for about half a minute, long enough to rattle every bone in his body and leave the horses half spooked.

"An earthquake," Maklin spat. "Damn, I hate this geyser country. The sooner I am shed of it, the better."

"Let's hope the Shakers are all right."

"Those idiots? It would serve them right if the earth opened up and swallowed them."

"Sure it would. You don't really want them dead."

"I am not you, Nate. I don't spare my enemies and I don't suffer fools."

They neared the mouth of the valley and drew rein in consternation. Borne on the breeze came screams and cries.

Chapter Sixteen

It was like riding into a nightmare.

Hissing steam rose from cauldron after cauldron. Pools of hot water were bubbling and roiling, some so violently that they spewed hot drops into the air. Part of the corral had broken and horses and mules were running loose. Oxen were milling and lowing. The wagons were undamaged but not the buildings. The roof on the female quarters had partly collapsed. So had the upright timbers on the building under construction and it now lay in ruins. People were scurrying every which way, Shakers and freighters alike. Wails of lament rose with the steam, as well as pleas for succor.

Nate brought the bay to a gallop. He swept past the freight wagons and the parked Conestogas and drew rein. Vaulting down, he ran to catch up to Jeremiah Blunt and Haskell and five other freighters who were running toward the female dwelling.

Blunt glanced at him. "You're just in time. The roof fell on some of the women. They need our help."

The doorway was clogged with female Shakers, many wringing their hands, some praying. Blunt shouldered through and Nate followed to where a crossbeam had cracked and come down. From under it jutted a woman's legs in a spreading scarlet pool.

"Good God!" Haskell exclaimed.

Farther in it was worse. Half the rafters had split in a large room where the women prepared meals. Nearly a dozen women had been in it when the earthquake struck. Some had been crushed to pulp. Others were alive but pinned by the weight of the fractured beams.

Arthur Lexington and other male Shakers had freed one young woman who was writhing in agony; from her knees down, her legs were splintered bone and mashed flesh.

Jeremiah Blunt barked commands and his men leaped to obey. They ran to the largest of the beams. Part of a woman was visible, her shoulder and arm and one leg, intact and untouched. Working quickly, the freighters put their backs to lifting the beam so Nate could get the woman out. Puffing and straining and grunting, they raised the massive weight by slow degrees. The instant it was high enough, Nate pulled. The woman came out from under easily enough, what was left of her.

One of the men turned away and retched.

Sister Amelia would never dance again. The timber had caught her across the top of her forehead and reduced it to a mush of brain and bone and hair. One eye had popped from its socket; the other had rolled up into her head, showing only the white. Her face was barely recognizable.

Nate looked away. He saw several Shakers trying to lift another beam and went to help. This time it was a young woman who had been pinned; her shoulder was shattered. She would live but be crippled for life.

The sobbing and wails, the smell of blood, the dust, and the gathering twilight lent a ghastly pall to the rescue efforts. Nate did what he could and after half an hour was caked with sweat, weary to his core, and sickened at heart. The last of the timbers had been moved. The last survivor rescued. When Jeremiah Blunt nudged him and motioned, Nate nodded and followed him out.

The cool night breeze was invigorating, for all of one breath. Nate sucked it into his lungs and wished he hadn't. A foul stench filled the valley, a reek like that of eggs gone rotten. Covering his mouth and nose, he breathed shallowly.

"I am not waiting for morning," Jeremiah Blunt declared. "I am gathering my men and leaving within the hour."

"I'm surprised you're not long gone," Nate said.

"Unloading took longer than I expected. I decided to stay over and leave first thing tomorrow." He gazed about them. "I'm glad I did. These people needed our help."

"They shouldn't be here."

"Perhaps between us we can persuade them it's in their best interests to pack up and get out before another earthquake strikes."

From out of the dark came Maklin. He was covered with dust and favoring his left leg. "I was over at that building they were putting up," he answered when Nate asked why. "Sprained my ankle helping to lift a beam." He took off his hat and ran a hand through his hair. "Five men are dead. Three others won't be walking for a while."

"It could have been worse," Blunt said.

Maklin tilted his head and went to put his hat back on, and froze. "What the hell *are* those things?"

Nate looked in the direction the Texan was staring. The pale specters had reappeared up near the caves high on the north side of the valley. Far more of them than the last time. They were larger, too. Coiling and writhing as before, they slowly oozed down the side of the mountain.

"Looks like fog or mist to me," Jeremiah Blunt said.

Nate agreed. It was rare to see fog that high up,

though. Usually fog clung to the valley floors. He put it from his mind. He had more important concerns. "Let's go talk to Lexington right this minute."

"Count me in," Maklin said.

The Shaker elder was at the hub of a score of Shakers. They were arguing heatedly. Lexington acted relieved when Blunt called to him.

"Did you hear them? My own people, saying I've been wrong and we should pack our wagons and leave Second Eden."

Nate said, "You can't stay, not after this."

Arthur Lexington sniffed. "It's a setback, is all. We will rebuild, make our buildings stronger. The brothers and sisters we have lost will be mourned and we will get on with our lives."

"Damn you," Maklin said.

"Here, now. I won't be addressed like that, Brother."

His hand a blur, the Texan seized Lexington by the front of his shirt. Nate went to intervene, but Jeremiah Blunt put a hand on his arm and shook his head.

"I'm no brother of yours and never want to be. How many of your followers died? Twelve? Fifteen? And you're so pigheaded, you won't take the rest out before the same happens to them."

Lexington smiled his benign smile. "Earthquakes are rare, Brother Maklin. You know that as well as I do. There might not be another for a thousand years."

"Or it could happen again tomorrow."

"Please, Brother." Lexington pried at the Texan's fingers. "I appreciate your concern. I truly do. But this display is unseemly. You must learn to trust in the Lord as I do."

Nate gazed toward the buildings. Torches had been lit and lanterns brought and the dead were being laid out in rows with blankets placed over them.

Cursing lustily, Maklin shook Lexington and drew back a fist as if to punch him.

"I would rather you didn't," Jeremiah Blunt said.

Reluctantly, Maklin lowered his hand—to one of his silver-inlaid pistols. "I should shoot him. It would be best for everyone."

"You wouldn't!" Arthur Lexington bleated.

"He won't," Blunt said.

Maklin gave Lexington a push that sent him stumbling against Nate, who caught him to keep him from falling. "Stay away from me, mister. I'm leaving with the captain and until then, come anywhere near me and I'll blow out your wick. So help me God." He turned and stalked off.

"My word," Lexington said. "What has gotten into the man? I can understand a fit of pique, but honestly now. He can't blame me for an act of nature."

Nate went after the Texan. He found him standing much too close to a hot spring. "Are you all right?"

"I haven't been all right since Na-lin died. I may never be all right again." Maklin tiredly rubbed his eyes and then pointed at the mountain to the north. "Have you noticed? It's a lot thicker now."

The fog or mist or whatever it was had spread. Many of the writhing tendrils had merged, coalescing into a large bank that was slowly creeping lower. For some reason it made Nate's skin crawl.

"In an hour or so it will reach here," Maklin observed.

"By then we'll be gone." Unnoticed, Jeremiah Blunt had come up behind them. Big hands on his hips, he stared somberly back at the laying out of the deceased. "There's no talking sense into that man. I thought maybe I could, being a Christian. I quoted Scripture. I reminded him we are our brother's keeper. I mentioned that God sends His rain on the just and the unjust. It did no good. He refuses to leave his Second Eden."

Maklin cussed and gestured at the boiling pool. "I should toss him in. No one will know. With him and Sister Amelia gone, the rest should be easy to convince."

"Two wrongs don't make a right."

Nate was watching the spectral bank. It enveloped everything in its path. He wondered why it was so pale.

"King? Did you hear me?"

Nate faced the captain. "Sorry. I wasn't listening."

"I'll be ready to leave within the hour. Are you coming with us? Or do you plan to stick around?"

Before Nate could answer, another tremor shook the Valley of Skulls. It wasn't as severe as the last, only a mild shaking that nonetheless set Nate's pulse to racing.

"Well, that does it," Jeremiah Blunt said, and made for the buildings. "Mr. Maklin, you're with me."

Nate listened to the bubbling of the hot spring. The rotten-egg smell was stronger. He held his hand over the lower half of his face as he trailed after them. A blanket was being draped over the body of Sister Amelia. Other Shakers were clustered in small groups and appeared to be arguing. The freighters were over by the corral, waiting for their boss.

Nate was suddenly homesick. He was filled with a great yearning to be with Winona, Evelyn, and Zach. If he slipped away now, under the cover of night, he could elude the Pawnees and be in King Valley in eight to ten days. His mind made up, he bent his steps toward the bay.

"Brother King! A word with you if you please."

Nate halted. The last person he wanted to talk to was Lexington. "Make it quick. I'm lighting a shuck."

"Are you indeed? That's a pity. I had a favor to ask." Lexington wagged the lantern he was holding toward the row of bodies. "We need to bury the departed as soon as practical."

"What's stopping you?"

Lexington leaned so close their shoulders brushed. "Have you ever heard the expression out of sight, out of mind? I prefer to bury them down the valley a ways. Since you were down there just the other day with Brother Maklin, I thought perhaps you would escort some of my people to a suitable spot."

Nate was puzzled. "You and the others must know this valley better than I do."

"To the contrary. We have been so busy organizing and building that there has been precious little time for exploring. I was to the end of the valley once, but that was months ago and I don't remember a blessed detail." Lexington lightly took hold of Nate's sleeve. "Please. It would only take an hour or two of your time and we would be ever so grateful."

Nate hesitated.

"I would ask Brother Maklin, but you've seen how he is when he's around me. I very much doubt he would help."

Nate heard himself say, "All right. Throw the bodies over horses and tie them so they won't fall off."

Lexington reacted as if he had been prodded with a sharp stick. "You can't be serious. That's no way to treat the departed. We'll load them in wagons. It won't take long, I assure you."

While the freighters were hitching their oxen, the Shakers hitched their mules. One by one the bodies were reverently carried to Conestogas and carefully placed inside. Nate figured one or two wagons was enough, but Lexington insisted on only putting three bodies in each. "After all, we don't want to cram them in like stacks of firewood, now, do we?" In all, it took five wagons. Lanterns were hung from each to help light the way.

Nate no sooner took the lead and bellowed for the drivers to head out than a young Shaker with curly corn-hued hair and white teeth came up alongside him, riding a sorrel.

"I'm to go with you, Brother King. I'm Brother Calvin. I'm very pleased to make your acquaintance."

Nate grunted.

"Brother Lexington wants me to sing over the bodies," Brother Calvin explained.

"Won't reading from the Bible do?" Nate wanted to get it done and get out of there.

"Oh, we'll do both. We must honor our brothers and sisters by showing the respect they deserve. After Brother Benedict reads, I'm to raise my voice to heaven, as Brother Lexington put it. I have a fine singing voice if I do say so myself. I should think four or five songs would be appropriate. Have you any suggestions?"

"It's not smart to stay there too long."

"What can happen? We'll be in the open. If there's another quake, it's not as if the sky will fall on us." Brother Calvin chuckled.

The dark hid Nate's frown as he reined wide of a boiling pool. Behind him, strung out in a row, the Conestagos creaked and rattled. Three of the five were driven by men. Women handled the other two.

"I envy Sister Amelia and the others," Brother Calvin remarked.

"You envy them being dead?"

"Oh, goodness no. I envy that when next they open their eyes, they will be in the throes of heavenly glory." Calvin lifted his rapturous face to the stars. "They are the lucky ones. We are still earthbound."

Nate looked up, too, and noticed that the roiling white bank was a lot lower and flowing a lot faster.

Chapter Seventeen

Brother Calvin didn't like the first spot Nate picked. "It's too near a hot spring. Those who come to pay their respects will have to put up with the stink."

Nate's uneasiness grew the farther they went. The fog or mist was a quarter of a mile above them when they came to a flat area within a stone's throw of the base of the mountain and far enough from any of the boiling springs and bubbling mud pots that Brother Calvin said it would do.

The Shakers brought lanterns and set to digging. The two women helped, sharing the work equally with the men.

Nate dismounted. He offered to lend a hand, but Brother Calvin told him they could manage on their own. Nate held the bay's reins and gazed down the valley at the lights and the activity. Jeremiah Blunt and the freighters were hitching teams and getting their wagons ready. In Nate's opinion Blunt was smart not to wait until morning.

Nate wished he could persuade Brother Lexington to do the same. The Indians had been right. The Valley of Skulls *was* bad medicine. No wonder they stayed away.

A pale gleam caught Nate's eyes. It was another skull. Larger than a buffalo's, it had a hole near the end of the jaw that might have been a horn. He wondered what sort of creature it could have been and what it died of.

Brother Calvin and the others finished one grave and began another. They weren't digging deep, only enough to keep scavengers from getting at the bodies.

Nate began to pace, the reins in his left hand. The bay clomped behind him, turning when he turned. He patted it and stared up the mountain. The ghostly bank was spreading ever lower.

Nate faced the Shakers. Almost too late he heard the smack of running feet, and whirling, he was just in time to raise his arm and ward off a blow that would have buried a knife in his chest. The Pawnee holding the knife howled and tried again.

Swiftly backpedaling, Nate leveled his Hawken. He thought it would be an easy kill, but the warrior knocked the barrel aside and was on him again in the bat of an eye. Nate drove the stock at the man's face, but the warrior nimbly darted aside.

Nate hadn't expected this. Not here, not now. He worried there might be more than this one warrior, that he'd get an arrow in the back, and had to resist the urge to look behind him. He focused on his attacker and only his attacker and when the Pawnee thrust at his stomach he unleashed a roundhouse that raised the man onto the tip of his toes and left him sprawled in an unconscious heap.

The Shakers ran over. Brother Calvin knelt next to the Pawnee and felt for a pulse. "He's still alive. Thank God you didn't kill him."

Nate would just as rather he did. He pointed the Hawken.

"What on earth do you think you're doing, Brother King?"

"Covering him while you tie him."

Brother Calvin put a hand to his throat as if appalled. "Oh, I could never do that."

"Why not?"

"It would be violence against my fellow man. We of the United Society of Believers in Christ's Second Appearing don't believe in violence. We are pacifists. Surely you know this."

"If he comes around he'll try to kill me again, and he might kill you while he's at it."

"I'm sorry." Brother Calvin shook his head and the other Shakers, who had hurried over, nodded in agreement.

"Fetch me a rope, then, and I'll bind him myself."

Brother Calvin grinned in amusement. "Were we to do that, it would be the same as binding him ourselves. I am afraid that any tying that must be done is yours to do."

"Don't you get it?" Nate asked. "Just becaue *you* don't believe in violence doesn't mean *he* doesn't. The world is full of men just like him who would as soon slit your throat as look at you."

"Honestly, now, Brother King," young Calvin said good-naturedly. "This is between the two of you. We have no quarrel with him or any of his tribe. To us, even the red man is our brother, and we will seek to live in harmony with them as we do with all living things."

"Life isn't the way you think," Nate said.

"That's beside the point. We live by our faith, not according to the ways of the world."

Nate opened his mouth to say the ways of the world would get them killed when his gaze fell on the slope above. The mist—for now that it was closer he could see that it was a vaporous mist and not true fog—was only a few hundred yards above them, devouring everything in its path. As he looked on it swallowed a cluster of pines.

Suddenly the bay nickered and pulled at the reins.

The mules started to act up, too. Some uttered loud whinnies that ended in brays. Some whimpered.

"What in the world?" Brother Calvin said, rising.

Nate hadn't taken his eyes off the mist. It was like white beads of sand suspended in the air. He had never seen anything like it. It rose a good twenty feet into the air and formed an unbroken white wall hundreds of yards across. "Get on your wagons and get out of here."

"What? Why? We haven't finished burying our brothers and sisters."

"That," Nate said, with a nod.

Brother Calvin looked, and laughed. "That mist or whatever it is? What harm can it do? For such a big man you are awfully timid."

One of the women anxiously wrung her hands. "I don't like that mist, either, Brother Calvin."

"You, too, Sister Edith?" Calvin chortled and moved toward his horse. "I'll prove to the both of you that your fears are groundless."

"Don't," Sister Edith said.

Nate echoed her. "I wouldn't do that if I were you."

Brother Calvin mounted and reined toward the mountain. "Watch and take heed." He jabbed his heels and trotted up the slope. When he was close to the mist he shifted to grin down at them. Holding his arms out from his sides, he hollered, "Now you will see how silly you've been."

One of the men said, "That's Brother Calvin for you. He sure is a character, isn't he?"

The mist swallowed more ground. Now it was almost on Calvin. They all heard his laugh as it closed over him like a shroud. For a few seconds there was silence. Then, from out of the mist, came a scream of pure bloodcurdling terror.

"My word!" a Shaker exclaimed.

"He's playing a trick on us," offered another.

"I'm not so sure," Sister Edith said.

Nor was Nate. He swung onto the bay and rode up the slope. Calling out Calvin's name, he came to a stop twenty yards from the mist. He thought he heard a soft hissing, but he wasn't sure. The bay whinnied and shied. "Easy, fella." Nate patted it. "Calvin?" he called out but got no answer. He reined around but didn't ride back down just yet.

Sister Edith was hurrying toward her wagon. The others were still by the Pawnee, who was stirring.

"Brother Calvin? Can you hear me?" Now only ten yards separated Nate from the mist. He peered into its depths but saw only white.

Then out lurched young Calvin. His hands were pressed to his fear-struck face. Mouth agape, he gasped and gurgled and made sounds Nate never heard a human throat utter. Calvin saw Nate and thrust out his hands in appeal. Then he screamed and pitched forward. A second more and the mist passed over him, hiding his twitching form.

Nate felt a spike of fear. The mist was almost on him. With a slap of his legs he flew toward the Conestogas. Sister Edith was on her wagon and attempting to turn it, but the other Shakers were rooted where they stood, transfixed by the horrific spectacle. "*Run!*" Nate bawled. They didn't have time to reach their wagons and rein the teams around.

The four of them broke into motion. But they didn't do as Nate had urged. Instead, they ran for their wagons.

"Run!" Nate tried again. He came to the bottom.

Sister Edith had her Conestoga around and it was lumbering off but oh so slowly.

Nate reined toward the other woman. She was almost to her wagon. Bending, he held out his hand and shouted, "Climb on behind me!"

The woman shook her head. Grabbing hold of the seat, she pulled her herself up and frantically began to goad her team.

Down off the mountain flowed the mist, silent save for the slight hiss that was like the hiss of steam and yet wasn't.

Nate got out of there. He galloped up to Sister Edith's Conestoga, ready to have her ride double with him if the mist overtook them. She turned on the seat to look back and he glanced around, too.

The Pawnee had sat up and was looking every which way in confusion. He saw the mist. With a sharp cry of fear he was on his feet and running, but he tripped after only a few steps and the mist poured over him. There was another piercing scream.

"Oh, God!" Sister Edith cried, and used her whip.

The white blanket was about to enfold the other Conestogas. One of the men had halted and faced it with his head high and his arms outspread. Exactly why eluded Nate. The mist closed about him and a shriek rent the night.

Two of the Conestogas were starting to turn and the last man was climbing onto his when the mist swept over them. This time there was a wail and a screech, and the mist flowed on.

"Ride with me!" Nate yelled to Sister Edith. Her Conestoga wasn't moving fast enough. The mist would overtake her.

She shook her head and went on urging her mules.

"You won't make it!"

Edith cracked the whip and bawled at her team. The Conestoga rolled faster, the wheels clattering over the rock, the bed swaying with every bounce. Edith glanced back again and smiled, apparently confident she could outrun the macabre destroyer.

"Look out!" Nate roared. She was making straight for a large hot spring. She heard him and saw her peril and wrenched to turn the team before it was too late— but it already was. With a terrible screech, the Conestoga swerved so sharply that two of its wheels came off the ground. The whole wagon tilted. It was going over. Sister Edith did the only thing she could. She sprang clear of the seat. But her leg caught, upending her, and instead of tumbling to the ground she did a complete flip—and landed in the hot spring.

With a rending crash the Conestoga came down on its side and rolled.

Nate reined toward the hot spring just as Sister Edith broke the surface. She screamed. Her face was blistered, her skin already being sloughed off like the leaves of boiled cabbage. Her eyes found his and she raised a beet-red hand. Then she went under a second and final time.

Nate galloped like a madman. It was nearly half a mile to the buildings. Behind him, borne by the wind, crawled the deadly mist, the Reaper in flowing white.

The freighters had been busy turning their wagons and lining them in a row. Nate figured that the racket explained why no one heard the screams. Most of the Shakers were standing around talking and were startled half out of their wits when he rode in among them bellowing at the top of his lungs.

"Run for your lives! Now! Or you are as good as dead!"

They all looked at him either in confusion or as if they thought he must be mad.

Arthur Lexington materialized, saying, "What is

this you're yelling about, Brother King? Why have you come back? I thought you were helping the burial party."

"They're dead."

"Who is?"

Bending, Nate grabbed Lexington by an arm and shook him, hard. "Listen to me. Do you see that mist?" Nate pointed. "It killed them."

An uncertain grin split Lexington's face. "You're joshing me, I take it? Since when is a mist deadly?"

"*This* mist is."

"I think you're pulling my leg."

Nate wanted to hit him. "You have maybe four or five minutes before it reaches here. Get your people out before it's too late." With that Nate raced to the freight wagons.

Jeremiah Blunt had heard the commotion and was at the last wagon in line, Haskell and Maklin on either side. "What's all the fuss about? Why all the shouting?"

Nate said, and got it out in as few words as possible, ending with, "Listen to me, Jeremiah. If you don't get your men out of here right this instant, you'll all die. Please believe me."

Jeremiah Blunt gazed down the valley. Unlike Arthur Lexington, he didn't scoff. "The mist, you say? He turned his horse and thundered for the wagons to move out. To Nate he said quietly, "Thanks for the warning. Are you coming with us?"

Nate jabbed a thumb toward the Shakers and shook his head.

"There are none so blind as those who will not see," Blunt said sadly, and spurred toward the head of the train.

Haskell nodded and followed.

That left Maklin. "I'll stick with you."

"Not this time."

"Give me one good reason."

"Lexington. Knowing you, you might shoot him."

"I might at that," the Texan admitted, a twinkle in his eyes. "Don't be long," he said, and galloped away.

Nate reined toward the buildings and couldn't believe his eyes. The Shakers hadn't moved. They were still standing around talking.

To the west the mist had spread and was bearing down on Second Eden.

Chapter Eighteen

Arthur Lexington turned as Nate vaulted from the saddle with the bay still in motion. Running up, Nate seized him and shook him as a riled bear might a marmot. "What in hell is the matter with you? I told you to get your people out of here."

Lexington indulged in his ever-ready smile. "Really, now, Brother King. Did you seriously expect me to believe your far-fetched claim? What do you take me for?"

It was the smile that did it. As eloquently as any words, it said that Nate was not only a liar but a fool and a simpleton. It nearly sent Nate berserk. He shook Lexington harder and drew back a fist to strike him, but at the last instant he shoved the man to the ground in disgust and turned to the startled and stunned Shakers. "Listen to me!" he cried, raising his arms. "You're in great danger." He pointed at the approaching pall of death. "That mist is poisonous. Breathe it and you die. I don't know how or why except maybe it comes out of the ground when the ground shakes. It will kill you if you don't flee. Get on your wagons. Get on your horses. *Now*."

Not one budged. They looked at one another in amazement or doubt and looked at the mist in puzzlement and finally one woman cleared her throat and with a sheepish grin said, "Is this a joke, Brother King? We know the Lord would never let anything like that happen to us."

"Please," Nate pleaded. "You're running out of time." The mist seemed to have slowed, but it was still inexorably advancing. "Brother Calvin and those who went to bury the bodies are dead. Do you want to end up like them?"

A man gazed up the valley. "Dead? Brother Calvin?" He faced his brethren. "There's only one way to prove if this man is trying to make a mockery of us." He went around the building and when he reappeared he was riding bareback. "I'll investigate," he announced, and brought his animal to a canter.

"Don't get too close!" Nate shouted. It was awful to stand there knowing the Shakers were squandering the precious minutes they needed to escape. He wanted to yell, to scream, to pound and prod them into fleeing.

The man on the horse wasn't much of a rider. He flapped and he flopped, but he stayed on. Then he was at the leading edge of the mist. Nate figured he would stop and call out to Brother Calvin and the others, but to Nate's astonishment the man did no such thing; he rode *into* the mist and was swallowed from view.

Nothing happened.

Nate waited for the scream sure to come, but none did. The Shakers were giving him looks that suggested they didn't approve of his jest. Then a big man with a voice that could carry far cupped a hand to his mouth and thundered, "Brother Simon! Have you found Brother Calvin?"

There was no answer.

Uneasiness began to spread. Nate took advantage by saying, "*Now* will you believe me? He doesn't answer because he can't. I beg you. Leave before it's too late."

Some of them started to move, but they stopped when Arthur Lexington strode past Nate and shouted, "Brothers! Sisters! Don't listen to this man. There is no such thing as poison mist. He wants us to leave because he thinks our coming here was a mistake."

"But the earthquake—" a man said.

"What about it? There might never be another here." Lexington moved among them, smiling and touching arms. "Are we to give up after so much effort? After we have come so far? After we worked for weeks to build our cabins? Are we to forsake Second Eden because of a quirk of Nature and this outsider?" He pointed at Nate. "Look at him. He's a mountain man. He has an Indian wife. He's lived among them for so long he's become part Indian himself. He thinks as they do. He takes their superstitions as true, but we know better, don't we?"

Nate barely held his simmering fury in check.

"The Indians think this is a bad place, so he thinks this is a bad place," Lexington had gone on. "He wants us to leave. The quake only made him more determined, so he concocts a ridiculous story about mist that kills." Lexington laughed merrily. "Have you ever heard anything so silly in your life?"

The mist had reached the green belt. Trees, grass, brush, all were being devoured.

Nate tried one last time. "I'm not the fool here. This man is. As God is my witness, I swear to you that what I've said is true. Please, *please*, if you value your lives, flee."

Lexington laughed louder. "Brothers and Sisters, do you know what I think? I think we should show our mountain man that he can't make fools of us. I think we should show him that our faith is the true faith." He gripped a woman's hand and held it high. "Do as I am doing. Link hands and form into a line. Hurry now, so we can prove him wrong and be shut of this nonsense."

To Nate's dismay, they did.

Arthur Lexington beamed and nodded and said words of encouragement, and when the line was formed, they stood facing the approaching mist, all with the same beatific smiles.

By then the mist was only a few hundred feet away. A mule that had strayed from the broken corral was nipping at grass and was covered in a matter of moments.

"See?" Lexington crowed. "Did that animal act panicked? It did not. Do we hear its death cries? We do not."

Nate ran to the bay and swung up.

"Raise our voices in song, brethren!" Arthur Lexington urged, and launched into "Rock of Ages."

Nate brought the bay to a gallop and didn't look back until he was past the cabins and the parked Conestogas.

The Shakers were still singing. Above them loomed the creeping shroud. They sang, and the mist flowed over them. For a few seconds the singing went on and then it abruptly stopped. From out of the mist came cries and yells and then the screaming began.

"The horror," Nate said. He stopped looking. The screams and shrieks went on and on. He would never forget them, not for as long as he lived.

The freight wagons had stopped outside the valley. Jeremiah Blunt and Maklin and Haskell were waiting. Blunt stared at Nate, the question in his eyes, and Nate shook his head.

"Damn."

"I tried my best. They wouldn't come."

"Don't blame yourself. Some folks just can't be reasoned with. Especially when they think they are right and the rest of the world is wrong." Blunt gave a toss of his head. "Well, then. Are you coming with us or going your own way?"

"My own," Nate said. He had his reason.

Each of them offered his hand in parting and when it was Maklin's turn, Nate glanced at his palm and said, "For me?"

"I have an extra and you might need it." Maklin smiled. "If you ever get to Texas look me up. My folks live in San Antonio."

"I just realized. You've never told me your first name."

"Marion."

"Marion Maklin?" Nate grinned.

"It's worse than that. Marion *Maurice* Maklin." The Texan sighed. "My pa was half drunk when he named me." He touched his black hat. "Take care, mountain man."

The freighters and their wagons melted into the night. Nate watched until they were out of sight. He was suddenly lonely. Reining into the forest, he rode until he came to a clearing. He climbed down, stripped the bay, and spread out his blankets. He lay on his back with a pistol in each hand and tried to sleep, but he kept hearing the screams and shrieks. An hour or so before sunrise he finally dozed off.

The chirping of finches woke him. Nate's stomach growled, but he ignored it and saddled the bay. He headed south, knowing it could happen at any time, the Hawken always in his hands. Noon came and went. By the middle of the afternoon he was having doubts until sparrows took noisy flight behind him.

Nate rode on. He was deep in the mountains he loved, the mountains he knew as well as he did the back of his own hand. The mountains were part of him and he a part of them. He was as much at home here as a city dweller on a city street. Here, he had the edge over the warriors out to count coup on him.

A ground squirrel scampered from his path, its bushy tail erect. A horned lark and its mate stared at him from a branch, the yellow of the male's throat as bright as a sunflower. A little farther on a hare went jumping in flight. In the winter it would be white, but now it was brown and blended into the brush.

Nate climbed until he was among white-bark pines. The nuts were a favorite with bears, both grizzlies and blacks. Squirrels cached them in cold weather. The trees grew to a height of sixty feet and were spaced well apart, exactly as Nate wanted. He ascended until he came to a boulder that jutted out of the earth like the jagged prow of a sunken ship. Reining behind it, he climbed down and let the reins dangle. He moved to a tree that afforded a view of the slope below, and hunkered.

Nate figured it wouldn't be long. His enemies were far from their own land and would want to end it sooner rather than later. The prairie was their home, not the mountains.

Two riders appeared, smack on his trail.

Nate had expected three. He watched behind them and scoured the woods to each side, but there were just the two unless one of them had circled ahead like the last time. That bothered him. He didn't want to have to watch his back.

The two below came closer. Kuruk was in front, his gaze glued to the bay's tracks.

Nate judged the time to be right. Cocking the Hawken, he stepped from under the pine. The pair whipped around but turned to stone when they saw his leveled rifle.

"So," Kuruk said.

"So," Nate replied.

"You are hard to kill, white-eye."

"I wanted to be left in peace," Nate said. "The blood that has been spilled is on your hands."

"My uncle's blood is on yours." Then Kuruk did a strange thing; he sat back and lowered his bow. Before we do what we must, I would ask a question of you."

"What?" Nate said suspiciously.

"The white cloud that kills. What is it? We were on the mountain to the south. We saw it cover Swift Owl and the whites and when it passed they were dead."

"I don't know what it was. It came from under the ground. To breathe it was to die."

"When I tell my people they will be much amazed. But they know I always speak with a straight tongue."

"You take a lot for granted."

Kuruk smiled. "You would not say that if you knew me better. I plan all that I do."

Nate wagged the Hawken. "Did you plan on this?"

"Yes, white-eye, I did."

Nate knew then. He had been right about the third warrior circling around. Shifting, he glanced out of the corners of his eyes but didn't see him.

Kuruk's smile widened. "I climbed a tree. I saw you ride around the big rock. When your horse did not come out the other side I sent Wolf's Claw on ahead." He switched to Pawnee and called out and from the woods behind Nate came a reply.

Nate was upset with himself. He had been so sure he could outfox them, and they had outfoxed him.

"Wolf's Claw has an arrow on you. If you try to shoot us he will put the arrow in your back."

"You want me alive," Nate said.

"I have always wanted you alive. The others who did not care as much, they only wanted you dead."

The warrior with Kuruk said something and Kuruk replied in anger and gestured sharply. "Did you hear him? Even now Bull Charging wants Wolf's Claw to kill you and have it done." His face hardened and he raised his bow, but he didn't draw back the string. "You will drop your rifle. You will hold your arms over your head while we take your pistols and your knife and tomahawk. You will do all this or you will die."

"You aim to kill me anyway," Nate said, and exploded into motion. He threw himself to the left and fired as he dived. An arrow flashed past, missing his shoulder by the width of a whang. He hit and saw Kuruk falling. Instantly, he grabbed for his pistols.

Bull Charging reined toward him and raised his lance. He hurled it just as Nate fired. The ball took the Pawnee high in the forehead and snapped his head back even as the lance thudded into the earth half an inch from Nate's chest.

Moccasins padded behind him.

Nate rolled and extended his other flintlock, but Wolf's Claw was already on him. A foot slammed his chin and a knee rammed his chest. Cold steel streaked in the sun. Nate jerked his neck aside and the blade sank into the dirt instead of his jugular. Thrusting the pistol against the warrior's ribs, he stroked the trigger. At the blast Wolf's Claw arched his back, clutched at the wound, and pitched over.

His jaw racked by pain, Nate rose to his knees. Both pistols and his rifle were spent. He reached for his powder horn and sensed rather than heard someone come up beside him. He tried to turn, but a blow to the temple felled him. Both flintlocks slipped from his grasp.

Kuruk reared over him. Kuruk's shirt was marked with red. There was red on Kuruk's tomahawk, too.

"I have you now, white-eye."

Nate's hand slipped under his buckskin shirt. He found his voice and said, "Your uncle."

It gave Kuruk pause. "What?" His tomahawk was poised for a final slash. "What about him?"

"He didn't leave me any choice, either." Nate pointed the pocket pistol Maklin had given him. It barely filled his hand but it was .70 caliber. The ball blew out Kuruk's right eye and much of the rear of his skull and Kuruk fell with a thump.

Nate slowly sat up. He touched the gash on his head. It wasn't deep and it wasn't bleeding much. He had been lucky. He would hurt for a while, but he would heal. Rising, he went about gathering their horses and then climbed on the bay.

He couldn't wait to get home

Author's Note

The entries in Nate King's journal having to do with Second Eden is the only known account of the fate of Elder Arthur Lexington and his splinter group of Shakers.

Some historians have questioned its authenticity. No Valley of Skulls has ever been found, the Indian legends notwithstanding.

But the Yellowstone region is famed for its many geysers and hot springs, and geologists say the area is highly unstable. Volcanic gases have been well documented. As has the fact that volcanic gases can be highly toxic.

So is Nate King's account true?

The author leaves it to the reader to decide.

The Classic Film Collection

The Searchers by Alan LeMay

Hailed as one of the greatest American films, *The Searchers,* directed by John Ford and starring John Wayne, has had a direct influence on the works of Martin Scorsese, Steven Spielberg, and many others. Its gorgeous cinematic scope and deeply nuanced characters have proven timeless. And now available for the first time in decades is the powerful novel that inspired this iconic movie.

Destry Rides Again by Max Brand

Made in 1939, the Golden Year of Hollywood, *Destry Rides Again* helped launch Jimmy Stewart's career and made Marlene Dietrich an American icon. Now available for the first time in decades is the novel that inspired this much-loved movie.

The Man from Laramie by T. T. Flynn

In its original publication, *The Man from Laramie* had more than half a million copies in print. Shortly thereafter, it became one of the most recognized of the Anthony Mann/ Jimmy Stewart collaborations, known for darker films with morally complex characters. Now the novel upon which this classic movie was based is once again available—for the first time in more than fifty years.

The Unforgiven by Alan LeMay

In this epic American novel, which served as the basis for the classic film directed by John Huston and starring Burt Lancaster and Audrey Hepburn, a family is torn apart when an old enemy starts a vicious rumor that sets the range aflame. Don't miss the powerful novel that inspired the film the *Motion Picture Herald* calls "an absorbing and compelling drama of epic proportions."

To order a book or to request a catalog call:
1-800-481-9191
Books are also available at your local bookstore, or you can check out our Web site **www.dorchesterpub.com**.

COVERING THE OLD WEST
FROM COVER TO COVER.

Since 1953 we have been helping preserve the American West
with great original photos, true stories, new facts,
old facts and current events.

True West Magazine
We Make the Old West Addictive.

Five-time Winner of the Spur Award

Will Henry

There is perhaps no outlaw of the Old West more notorious or legendary than Billy the Kid. And no author is better suited than Will Henry to tell the tale of the young gunman . . . and the mysterious stranger who changed his life.

Also included in this volume are two exciting novellas: "Santa Fe Passage" is the basis for the classic 1955 film of the same name. And "The Fourth Horseman" sets a rancher on the trail of a kidnapped young woman . . . while trying to survive a bloody range war.

A BULLET FOR BILLY THE KID

ISBN 13: 978-0-8439-6340-3

☐ **YES!**

Sign me up for the Leisure Western Book Club and send my FREE BOOKS! If I choose to stay in the club, I will pay only $14.00* each month, a savings of $9.96!

NAME: _____

ADDRESS: _____

TELEPHONE: _____

EMAIL: _____

☐ I want to pay by credit card.

☐ VISA   ☐ MasterCard   ☐ DISCOVER

ACCOUNT #: _____

EXPIRATION DATE: _____

SIGNATURE: _____

Mail this page along with $2.00 shipping and handling to:
**Leisure Western Book Club
PO Box 6640
Wayne, PA 19087**
Or fax (must include credit card information) to:
610-995-9274

You can also sign up online at **www.dorchesterpub.com.**

*Plus $2.00 for shipping. Offer open to residents of the U.S. and Canada only.
Canadian residents please call 1-800-481-9191 for pricing information.
If under 18, a parent or guardian must sign. Terms, prices and conditions subject to change. Subscription subject to acceptance. Dorchester Publishing reserves the right to reject any order or cancel any subscription.